The Bishop of Mars

by Steven Charleston

RED MOON PUBLICATIONS
Oklahoma City, OK 73120

This book is a work of fiction. Names, characters, places, and incidents either are products of the author's imagination or are used fictitiously. Any resemblance to actual events or locales or persons, living or dead, is entirely coincidental.

Cover Art by Suzanne (Susan) Charleston, www.suzanneartist.com

Book Layout by Lana B. Callahan, www.lbsdesignstudio.com

Library of Congress Control Number: 2013911622
ISBN 978-0-9851419-3-6

Printed in the United States of America

DEDICATION

FOR SUSAN
whose life is art.

Prologue

Writing this book was Digby's idea. Without his permission, especially since it would reveal who he is, I would never have written it. But he says it could be "of great historical significance". So here it is.

It is the story of how I became the Bishop of Mars. It explains all of the things that happened shortly after I arrived, things that are still happening in many ways as those events keep changing life on Mars.

I hope I have told the whole story. It all happened very fast and I do have troubles with my memory because of my old addiction to Zap. Digby said to put my Zap-dreams into the story. I thought that might be confusing, but Dr. Wu says they are "essential for filling in the negative space", so I wrote them in as part of what I experienced.

I don't know who may read this book in the years to come, so I try to explain a little about the reality of life now…on Home World, in West Hem, and on Mars…just in case things have changed a lot in the future and people forget what life was like in our time.

What we discovered on Mars will probably mean that the future will be very different from anything we have known before. It could mean that nothing in reality will ever be the same.

Bishop Anthony of Mars
2745 AD (After Drought)

The Bishop of Mars

Chapter One

"Mars is the garden of Eden."

The woman across the table from me gave me a quizzical look.

"Do you mind if I write that down?" she asked.

I took another bite of my salad.

"No, I don't mind," I said.

We were in the dining car of the Crown Prince Jianyu on our way to Mars. I was flying coach so I had to share a table. My dining partner on this evening was Esther Kaminski from Saint Petersburg. She took a small portable ComCom from her purse and started pushing buttons.

"It is a nice image," she smiled at me, "I could use that. Tell me more about what it means to you."

She looked at me expectantly. Her pale blue eyes were set deep in a broad face beneath eyebrows that seemed like two pencil lines drawn across white paper.

"Well," I said, "from what I have heard Mars is like a new creation. It is an unspoiled garden. It is turning green. Coming alive."

"Yes," Esther said enthusiastically as she typed away with her thumbs, "It is coming alive while Earth is dying."

"I guess so," I said. I watched her make some more notes, then asked her the obvious question. "But why are you writing this down? Are you a writer?"

Esther put her ComCom back in her bag and nodded.

"I am going to Mars because of demographics," she said.

"I'm sorry," I said, "My Russian isn't so good. What was that last word?"

"Demographics," she repeated slowly, " People. Right now most of the people living on Mars are still the rough and tumble types. You know…miners, factory workers, terraformers. It's still a frontier. But all that is changing. Did you know that last year the number of tourists going to Mars increased by almost ten per cent?"

I shook my head, "No, I had no idea."

"Given the cost of travel, almost all of those who made the trip would be considered your first class traveler."

"So Mars is a growing travel market?"

"Exactly," she smiled, "That's why I am writing a book about it. Next Stop, Mars. That's what it will be called."

"Oh, the Next Stop books," I said, "I've heard of those. Next Stop, Tibet. Next Stop, Antarctica."

"Next Stop, Greenland," she continued, "I've written all those."

I leaned back in my chair and took a sip of tea.

"I am impressed. You must have traveled all over the place."

"Every major destination in the Twin Empires and the African Free States," she said proudly.

"Have you ever been to West Hem?"

She stopped lifting her chopsticks halfway to her mouth and frowned.

"I'm sorry," she said, "I don't mean to offend you, but that's not really the kind of travel I write about."

"No offense taken," I said quickly, "I understand. I was just wondering if you had ever been there."

"No," she said a little stiffly, "I have never been."

We ate for a moment in silence. She patted her lips with a napkin.

"I could tell by your accent that you are from West Hem," she said carefully, "but I must say you don't seem like any of the men I have met from a Vegas city."

"I will take that as a compliment," I said.

"I meant it as a compliment," said Esther Kaminski, "You don't look anything like a Vegas lawyer."

"So what do I look like?"

She tilted her head to look at me.

"No gold chains," she said slowly, "No gold teeth…"

She reached over with one hand to slightly touch my chin, turning my head into the candlelight.

"No surgical enhancements. Dark hair. Grey eyes. Probably Irish by background and around fifty." Esther seemed pleased with her analysis of my looks. "Just a nice honest face with kind eyes. You look like my Rabbi. Except for the Irish part."

I laughed.

"What is so funny?" she asked, "Am I wrong?"

"No," I said, "not wrong. In fact, almost too right."

Esther Kaminski gave me another quizzical look.

"I'm not a Rabbi," I explained, "but close. I'm a priest. A Christian priest. I am going to Mars to be the bishop of Mars."

"No," she said, "I don't believe it."

"It's true," I said, "I am a bishop."

Esther drew her full lips up into a small frown.

"You are a Christian priest and you are from West Hem?"

I nodded.

"No," she drawled, "It is not possible. There are no Christians in West Hem. No Jews or Muslims, either. That is what they say in Russia. No religion could exist in this kind of place."

I shrugged, "What better place for religion than where it is needed the most?"

Despite what Esther had heard, there are religious people in West Hem. It's just that they aren't easy to see under all the glitz and glitter of The Vegas pleasure cities. In fact, you could say that The Vegas saved religion in West Hem. Once the old world was swept away by the Drought, the chaos brought on by famine and war was finally settled by the rise of the Twin Empires. The Tsar in Russia and the Emperor in China. But in the western hemisphere, in West Hem, things took a different turn. The collapse of the old civilization left a vacuum. The Vegas filled that vacuum. They did not seek to compete with the Twin Empires, but rather, to pander to them. The lords of The Vegas, the bosses of bosses, created an economy of procurement. On the foundation of crumbling cities, from Boston to Buenos Aires, they constructed a series of pleasure cities. Casinos, night clubs, race tracks, drug of choice emporiums, brothels with every form of sex tourism: if the Drought left Earth with a global hangover, The Vegas had the cure. While the Twin Empires went about the business of running the world, The Vegas went about the business of giving them a place to let off steam. Now Russia and China look the other way as their bankers and bureaucrats, aristocrats and nouveau riche, come to The Vegas party towns for all the pleasures they cannot indulge at home. Sex tourists, gamblers, high rollers and the rich and famous, they all mingle in West Hem, where everything is for sale if you have the money.

As this new reality expanded across West Hem, many people junked religion all together and got on the fast track with The Vegas. But others fell off that track...or were pushed...into an alternative. Gamblers with nothing left to bet on but God, sex workers tired of trying to pretend they were having fun, chambermaids fed up with cleaning toilets: the converts of a religious renaissance.

I was one of them.

I was an addict when I found religion. I had been selling Zap when I was thirteen. By the time I was fifteen I was both selling and using. At twenty, I was just using. I tried to steal what I could not buy. I got caught and had what was left of my body beaten into hamburger. I wound up in a charity ward. If Esther Kaminski had been writing my biography it would have been called, Next Stop, City Morgue. Fortunately, or by divine intervention, depending on how you look at it, she was not the author of my salvation. Ima Clare was.

Clare is a Two-Fer. A Sunflower. A Psy-clone.

As a kid, she had been a little girl growing up poor on the chain of islands that used to be Florida. She had been handed off to the local Vegas boss to cover gambling debts and wound up being used in experiments to transfer a human mind from one brain into another. A Two-Fer...two for the price of one. In her case, or his case as it came to be, this had been into the brain of an older man, a guy working construction jobs who just happened to be in the wrong place at the right time when The Vegas was out trolling for candidates to clone.

In those days, The Vegas doctors really didn't care who they mixed up. Women into men, men into women, kids into old people, all races, all ages...it didn't matter to them. They were trying to perfect the process. That's all that mattered. That process is illegal in the Empires but still being tried by The Vegas because one day it may provide the ultimate big ticket item: immortality. People would pay a lot for immortality, for the ability to have their mind, their personality transferred from a dying body into a new, healthy, young body. So The Vegas keeps working on the formula. The fact that they haven't succeeded is demonstrated by the reality that almost all Psy-clones are severely schizophrenic. The name Psy-clone is a joke because people like Clare have emotional cyclones in their brains. Not the kind of immortality that is very marketable. Only a few Psy-clones have managed to balance their personalities. Clare is one of them.

You can tell that Clare is a Psy-clone because she has yellow eyes. Black pupil, yellow iris: Sunflower. That's another side effect of The Vegas process. It turns the iris of the human eye a bright and distinctive sunflower yellow. It was a pair of these yellow eyes that welcomed me back to the land of the living when I woke up in the charity ward.

"Where am I?" were my first words.

"Well, you are not in heaven," Ima Clare had said.

"So what does that mean? Am I in hell?"

"Close enough," she laughed, "You are back in Pilgrim's Playground."

In those days, Clare was a nun working in the public hospitals. These are not the high end private clinics that do bio-enhancements for the wealthy. These are the wards for the poor...acute melanoma patients, consumption cases, trauma victims...and of course, the garden variety Zappies like me...addicts...cadavers posing as people. It is not the kind of work many people line up for, so when Clare first wandered in to the convent, asking to join the Sisters, they didn't mind that it was an African man with a young woman's voice and bright yellow eyes. They saw past that to the person within. Or in Clare's case, to the people within.

Clare stayed by me. She made sure I got enough sub-Zap to keep me from climbing the walls. She fed me, washed me, and talked to me until I could function on my own. But the thing I remember most is that she prayed for me.

Late at night, when the ward was just a pool of light around my bed, I would rise up out of my dream state (deep dreaming is a by-product of Zap) to find her sitting on a little metal chair mumbling prayers next to me. I never actually heard what she was saying. It was just the fact that she was doing it.

Praying. For me.

No one had ever done that before. No one had ever cared to.

When I got out of the ward I didn't go back to the street. I went to work at her Convent. It was a rundown old house with bad plumbing, a leaky roof, and lots of novice cockroaches. Saint Firetrap's we called it.

I helped cook the meals while the Sisters were out bandaging up the poor. I did the odd jobs that were always in demand to keep the place from caving in. I slept in a room by the kitchen. Each morning and evening, I would stand in the back of their creaky-floor chapel while the Sisters said their prayers. I learned all of those prayers by heart. I can still say them today.

"Lucky, do you have a minute?"

I looked down from my ladder to see Ima Clare's yellow eyes looking up at me from beneath her straw hat.

"Hang on, Sister, just let me get these awnings fastened. Got to keep the sun out."

"You shouldn't be out here without a hat anyway," she said, "you know the rules. Get down and come inside, I want to talk to you."

I hammered in the last nail and climbed down. I found her sitting in the chapel alone. Not a good sign. The chapel was always the place for serious talks.

"What did I do?" I asked as I sat down next to her. "I was wearing sunblock."

Clare smiled at me, smiled that patented smile of hers. Her face was that of a grown man. Her voice was that of a young woman. But her smile...that was like nothing else you have ever seen. Even if you were dying, it would bring you back to life.

"This isn't about sunblock," she said, "it's about you."

I swallowed. Definitely not a good sign.

"I ate the bananas," I blurted out.

"What?"

"The bananas. I ate them. I confess."

"It's not about bananas, either," she smiled again, "it's about you going to the Farm."

Down the hall, in the silence of St. Firetrap's on a quiet afternoon,

I heard the wall clock strike two, a time I will always remember since it was at that exact hour that my journey to becoming a bishop began.

"The Farm? You want me to go to the Farm?"

Clare nodded.

"Are you sure prison might not be easier for me? Why don't you send me there instead?"

Clare laughed. I leaned back in my chair, listening to that young sound come out of a grown man's body. I didn't get the joke.

The Farm is a commune out in the Dry Lands. It is a working farm trying to pull life out of the desert. It is where people go to sweat for five years to see if they can become priests in the Common Prayer Church. If you make it, they change your name to a saint's name. You become an Abba if you are a male priest or an Ima if you are a female priest. Ima Clare had called me down from the ladder with my street name, Lucky, something I picked up from a gambler who once threw me a tip for bringing him luck when I was a kid. Now she was pointing me toward the wilderness where I would become something new.

"You have to be kidding," I said, "I can't do that. I'm not cut out for that. Oh no, not me. That's crazy. I'm a Zappie, for God's sake."

"You were a Zappie," Clare said, "but now you are free. Look at how far you have come in two years. All the Sisters say so."

"Sure, but they are Sisters, so what would you expect? But you know I am not good enough to do what you do. I'm not good enough to be a priest. That's a crazy idea."

"None of us are good enough to be what we become," she said quietly, "that's why we need God."

Ima Clare stood and smoothed the skirt of her habit. She placed one large hand on my shoulder.

"Pray about it," she said, "that's all we are asking. We have watched you over these years, Lucky. We have seen the goodness, the kindness, in you. You can do so much more than just odd jobs around this place. You can do the work of God and this world needs all the help it can get. We think you would be a fine Abba for the church. So please, just pray about it."

She walked away, leaving me sitting by myself in the buttery light of the late afternoon, sitting in the chapel where I had heard so many prayers before. I looked at the worn wooden table that was the altar. How could anyone think I ought to be a priest? The bent cross on the altar leaned a little to the left. Why would the Sisters want to send me away? The sunflowers in a tin can next to the cross had started to droop. Why would God want me? I kept looking at the altar. I started my prayer with only one clear thought: "I ought to fix that cross and change that water."

I know why they change your name when you become a priest. I went to the Farm as a smartass kid named Lucky and I came out as a much wiser man named Anthony. The Farm changed me.

The Farm (the real name is Sanctuary, but most students call it Boot Camp) is on the edge of the Dry Lands, the outback interior of the northern part of West Hem. Most people who live in the pleasure cities think the Dry Lands are an unpopulated wilderness, but there are a lot of people who live out there. It is not an easy life, but at least it's a much freer one. The Vegas doesn't pay much attention to the Dry Lands. You can get lost in the desert, and sometimes that's a good thing.

When I was a student at the Farm the Abbess was a tough old woman named Hannah, a small woman in patched overalls and a straw hat who seemed twice her size if she caught you goofing off. The Farm is always run by a man or woman who is not a priest, a lay person, either an Abbot or Abbess of Sanctuary. Abbess Hannah was in charge of a community of around a thousand people all together. Many were families living along the irrigation canals on small farm plots. They fed themselves from what they raised and contributed the surplus that the Farm then sold to the cities to pay for equipment and supplies. Others lived in the main part of Sanctuary, a communal village working large fields, greenhouses, and aqua beds. There were the few of us who were novice priests, men and women sent by their home communities to be trained in the discipline of a spiritual life. Those who were married lived with their own families in small cottages; single students like me lived in a dorm beside the main church.

Our teachers were called the Elders. Each Elder was responsible for a different part of the Farm (the irrigation canals, the orchards, the communal kitchen) and they were each responsible to teach us a different subject as we worked for them. So I learned about our sacred books when I was milking cows, about ethics when I was cleaning the bath house toilets, about history when I was digging canals.

During the day I would be working and listening, during the night I would be reading. At both times, I was expected to be praying.

"Work is prayer," Abbess Hannah used to say, "study is prayer, prayer is prayer. There is no beginning or ending. Just doing. It's all the same. That's life."

It was at the Farm that I learned to read and write. I couldn't be writing this if it wasn't for what they taught me. I had not gotten much education growing up in Pilgrim's Playground. The Vegas is not big on educating people who cannot serve them with some profitable research or technology, so I had a lot of catching up to do. Each week I would spend any free time I had at the Farm's library, practicing reading, practicing writing. Like most city people, I knew a little Chinese and Russian, but I could neither read nor write in Hemish. Part of the work of the Farm is to translate old books into our language or to write new ones. These are printed out on the paper we made from canal reeds. Unlike city schools, we did not depend on ComCom tablets because, as Elder Thomas, our chief librarian, was fond of saying, "The Vegas owns the ComCom but God owns the Word." So printed words are making a comeback in the Dry Lands where people can think what they want, write what they want, and read what they want without fear of being watched.

"So how many religions are there?"

Elder Michael, our history teacher, and I were taking a break from repairing one of the windmill pumps near the corn fields.

"Enough to go around," he laughed. "The world is full of religion these days. In China there are Confucians and Buddhists. In Russia there are the Orthodox. Those are the two big religions, the official religions I guess you would say. And then there are Jewish and Muslim people spread around. A lot of them had to leave the Med Marshes after the sea there dried up and now they live in the Twin Empires or the African Free States."

"How about here?"

"Here? In West Hem?" he looked at me from the corner of his eye and smiled, "You mean aside from money?"

"Yes, aside from money."

"Well, we have all of the above, of course, and then we have our own brand of Christians. What do you remember about them?"

I was glad to have a few more minutes in the shade so I tried to recite an answer that would keep us talking.

"There is our church, the Church of Common Prayer. We come from an old church that started in England over a thousand years ago. There are the Apocalyptics who think the Drought happened because God wants to punish us. There are three kinds of Catholics. They all believe the same thing, but can't agree about which of the three Popes is the real one. There are the Protestant Union churches who think they know when the Earth will be healed. The Baptizers, who want to save the people in the cities from a life of sin. I guess that's about it."

Elder Michael was nodding under his farm hat, although whether in agreement with what I had said or from feeling lazy in the shade I could not tell. We sat quietly for a while. The desert breeze pushed the windmill around to play its creaky metal tune and draw water from deep below us. A bee from one of the Farm hives buzzed past us.

"But which one is right?" I asked him.

Elder Michael stretched his long legs and then got slowly to his feet. He looked out over the army of green corn that stood at attention beneath the sun.

"The one that is right for you," he said. Then he picked up his wrench and looked at me. "Any other answer would assume we know more than God. So just be true to what you believe and let the others believe what they believe. In the end, it will be up to God to sort out the rightness of the thing. We aren't in the business of judging people. That's not our job."

"So what is our job?" I asked.

"Fixing this pump," he said, "that's our job."

And so we did.

Abbess Hannah gave me my name at the big party the Farm celebrated each year when students had finished their five years and were ready to go home to be ordained. Beneath strings of colored lights, under the endless vault of the desert sky, beside long tables covered with the food we had raised together, the people of Sanctuary gathered to feast the new beginning and honor the old story. One by one, Abbess Hannah called us forward to receive the simple white shell choker that we would wear as a sign of our office.

"Lucky," she said, "you are now going to be called Anthony." She placed the shells around my neck. "Wear your name proudly. Like you, Anthony was a man with a past who found his future out in the desert. But first, he had to fight off a lot of demons. We figure that you have fought off Zap, and that's one of the biggest demons we face these days. So from now on, you will be Abba Anthony. Go back to Pilgrim's Playground. Work hard. Pray hard. And try to have some fun along the way."

The next morning I left Sanctuary, left the Farm, having completed my boot camp. I had my shell choker in my bag, a copy of the Hemish Bible, and a holopix of my graduating class. I also had a stronger body, a lot more patience, a deeper wisdom and a better sense of humor. Like my namesake, I had left a lot of my demons in the desert. I still had my Zap dreams some nights, but I wasn't haunted by so many of the old memories of life on the streets.

During my five years of study I had gotten to see Ima Clare only once. The Sisters at St. Firetrap's don't have much money so they could only afford for one of them to make the trip out to the Dry Lands. I was glad it was Clare. She had shown up one hot summer day when the air was so still you could feel it on your shoulders. Abbess Hannah had given me time off to be with her. When I first saw her I had run like a kid to his mother, almost jumping up to be held in the bear hug of her powerful arms. Clare is much larger than me. She has the body of a man who worked outside, broad shoulders, strong arms, big hands. I asked her about him while we sat in rocking chairs on the porch of the dining hall, watching distant clouds float over sleeping fields.

"His name is Clarence," she said, "That's why the Elders gave me the name of Clare when I came through the Farm. Because Clarence and I share the same body we sort of share the same name."

"Is he still there?"

"Yes. He is. Clarence is always there. In the beginning, when I was still a little girl, it was kind of scary waking up in the body of a giant, but Clarence is a gentle giant. He helped me feel safe. He helped me grow and become myself. He even told me stories at night before I slept. Now he just stays in the background, like he is sleeping. He only emerges when we are alone, or when things are stressful, or when I am angry. Then he shows up."

"Is that bad?"

"No, not bad at all. Clarence and I talk. He always has good advice.

He has helped me so much. In fact, he is listening to us right now."

"I can't imagine what that must be like."

"Not many people can," Clare said, "in fact, it made me quite a challenge for the Elders to handle when I was here."

That surprised me. I always thought of Ima Clare as next to perfect.

"You didn't goof off or sneak into the kitchen at night, did you?"

"No, not that kind of challenge," she laughed, "I was a spiritual problem for them to solve." Clare shifted her large frame around in the rocking chair so she could reach the pitcher of cold green tea that sat on a little table between us. She poured more into each of our glasses and then explained, "I am two people in one body. I am two genders. I am two different ages. So, in the end, what am I? Am I a human being? Or two human beings? Am I a man or a woman? Am I a child or an adult? Do I have two souls or one soul? Could Clarence die before me? Or will we die together? And, if we did, would we stay together in the next life or be separated?"

"I have no idea," was all I could think to say.

Ima Clare rocked back, laughing her gentle child-like laugh, "Neither did they."

We watched the clouds in silence for a moment, happy for the shade of the porch, happy to be sitting together.

"Hey, I have another thought," I said finally, "another problem for the Elders." Clare looked over at me. "Who did they ordain? You or Clarence? Or both of you? Is he ordained too?"

Ima Clare reached up to touch the shell choker around her neck.

"Good question," she said, "I never thought of it that way, but since the Elders always make us tell them what we've heard, I will give you my answer. I think it was both of us. I think Clarence shared in this whole experience at the Farm with me. I think he became a nun with me. And I think he is a priest with me. We may be different people, but he has always let me take the lead. He has come along for the ride. And because he has done that for me, I have tried to do something for him."

"What's that?"

Ima Clare looked down at the two size 14 shoes sticking out from under habit.

"I have stayed in his body. I have never gotten the change. Never even asked him for it."

"Maybe one day it will be alright with him."

In the distance the bell rang for evening prayers. We both stood up. I took a last drink of cold tea.

"Maybe," she said, "but that's up to him, not me. For now, I will be content to be the only nun who can do this…" and she picked me up and carried me over her shoulder, both of us laughing, halfway across the yard.

The night before we landed on Mars I remembered that conversation. I was sitting in a chair in the lounge, watching a group of Chinese businessmen playing Mahjong. My mind was drifting back over all the years since I had been at the Farm, as if those memories were a lifeline still connecting me to Earth. And it was not just the happy memories that I carried with me to Mars, but the hard ones as well. In the twentieth year of her ordination Clare had been put forward by her Order to become a bishop in the Common Prayer Church. That suggestion started a fight in the church that nearly brought St. Firetrap's down.

When the Sisters of Hope, Clare's religious Order, sent her to the Farm a lot of people in the church objected. Just like we had talked about on the porch, they were full of questions that were hard to answer. Was Clare really a person or were Two-Fers something other than human? Was she an Abba, an Ima, or both? That was bad enough, but when it came to electing her a bishop, the arguments became violent.

In the end, she was approved by a majority of the people in our church, but an angry minority of church members rejected her as too "un-human" for the job. A sizeable number of people left the church because of her, or rather, because of their fear of her. And yet, Clare, and I suppose Clarence, proved the truth of their calling over the next five years because she was such a good bishop. Her care for all of us who served under her as priests, her constant work on behalf of the poor, her courage in facing up to The Vegas in its worst abuses of power, all of these things are part of my memories of Earth. They are an explanation for why I would do anything for her, even cut off my finger, which is what I almost did when she asked me to go to Mars.

"Mars?"

"That's right. Mars".

We were sitting on stools in the kitchen at St. Firetrap's. I had been cutting up potatoes for a soup. When Ima Clare, now Bishop Clare, had asked me if I would consider going to Mars my hand slipped and I cut my finger.

"You have to be joking."

"No, I mean it. In another month, after Archbishop Jerome retires, the West Hem bishops are going to elect a new head of the church. Whoever they elect will get to name the new missionary bishop of Mars. If I win, I want it to be you."

"Me? A bishop?"

Clare nodded as she put a bandage on my finger.

"But don't worry," she said, "my chances of winning are really small. After all of the outrage when I became a priest, and then the freak out when I became a bishop, I doubt they will want to stir up more trouble by making me the Archbishop."

"But what if they do?"

"Then I get more hate mail and you get to go to Mars," she smiled.

Joan of Arc was cutting carrots in the kitchen. She was wearing a fleur de lis tunic over her chain mail. I was peeling potatoes.

"Damn," she said, sucking her finger.

"What happened?"

"I cut myself," she said, "I got distracted. I wasn't paying attention."

"What's the matter?" I went around the table to look at her finger.

"Oh, the usual," she said, "I keep hearing voices in my head."

I rummaged in a drawer, looking for a band-aid.

"Do you think I'm crazy?" she suddenly asked.

I peeled back the band-aid and started putting it on her finger.

"No," I said, "You are not crazy. You are an inspiration to millions."

She held up her finger in the sunlight.

"But at what cost?" she said, "How much blood has been spilled because of me?"

"That's not your fault," I said going back to my potatoes, "People are just afraid of what they don't understand."

Saint Joan laughed.

"Boy, have you got that right," she said, "Why do you think I wear armor?"

I stood at the baggage claim waiting for my luggage. The bags slid down a chute onto a revolving conveyor. I was standing next to scores of other people, people from many different parts of the Twin Empires. Some were immigrants, Chinese or Russian couples with children, relocating to Mars, their kids straining to be released onto a new world, tugging at the hands that held them. There were single men and women like me, coming to start new jobs. They would work in the growing Martian economy as terraformers, geologists, miners, construction workers, or in one of the greenhouse gas factories. On Mars the same halocarbon gases that helped create the Drought are intentionally put into the atmosphere because as the planet warms the oxygen and water trapped beneath the surface are released. What killed Earth is giving life to Mars.

Esther Kaminski passed by, pushing her bags on a cart.

"Good luck, Rabbi," she said happily, "Next Stop, Mars."

"I'll look for the book when it comes out," I called after her.

My bag finally appeared. I hadn't brought much. Just about the same things I took with me when I left the Farm. My Hemish Bible. My shells. A holopix of Clare and the other bishops gathered around me on the day they consecrated me to be the new bishop of Mars.

They looked happy. I looked stunned.

I picked up my bag and headed toward Customs.

"There is no beginning or ending. Just doing."

Abbess Hannah's words came back to me as I pushed open the swinging doors into the Mars Space Terminal.

"That's life," I said out loud.

Chapter Two

Welcome to Burroughs Base.

The sign was in the three languages of Earth: Chinese, Russian and Hemish. I joined the line of passengers shuffling down the ramp to Customs and Immigration. There are many names for Martian towns. Most are Chinese or Russian, of course. There are lots of "news": New Shanghai, New Kiev, New Moscow, New Hong Kong. But the largest town is Burroughs Base, named after a writer most people have forgotten.

It was teenagers who saved him. Teenagers with a lot of time on their hands. The affluence of the Chinese Empire had filled Tiananmen Square with the sons and daughters of bankers who were looking for the next outrageous option to express their hormonal creativity. With the Mars colonization project in the news they turned to the ancient past and dug up the novels of Edgar Rice Burroughs. His Martian series of melodramas became the fashion. Each Saturday Tiananmen Square was filled with Chinese boys and girls dressed in the leather harnesses and skimpy thongs of John Carter and Deja Thoris, the icons of Edgar Rice Burroughs soap opera Mars. It drove their parents nuts, which was the main idea. The sober Confucian revival of the Empire was the perfect cultural Petri dish to grow the adolescent rebellion of near naked Chinese kids acting out the fantasies of an imaginary Mars.

The fad passed. The kids grew up. But by the time the joint Chinese-Russian colonization project was literally off the ground, these teenagers were the technocrats making it happen. They had traded in their thongs for lab coats but they never forgot the icon of their youth. When the first Chinese-Russian explorers set down on the Red Planet they diplomatically dubbed the landing site by the neutral name Burroughs Base. It is not a name partial to either of the two great languages and that signifies the careful compromise between the two superpowers that made the whole project work. Edgar would have been proud.

"Do you have anything to declare?" The Russian speaking customs agent who asked me this question must have been close to seven feet tall. He was dressed in the black overalls of the Mars Central Authority, the administrative government of Mars that runs things for the Twin Empires.

"No, nothing", I said in Russian.

"You have no agricultural products in this bag?" he asked, looking at me with a doubtful expression that all customs agents must practice in a mirror.

"No, none," I answered.

He paused to look at me. He squinted. I swallowed.

"Next," was all he said.

I lifted my travel bag and walked out to the arrival lobby. It did not look anything like I had imagined. In my mind I had seen Mars as a frontier of prefab. I expected corrugated tin-like structures with exposed wiring and metal floors. Instead I saw a Roman bath house. The lobby was a series of vaulted ceilings, all made of brick, rising from a sand colored stone floor. The vast cavern was supported by sculpted columns of pink stone, with fluted cornices. In the center of the terminal was a rectangular pool of water. It had a globe of Mars in red stone as a fountain. A many colored tile mosaic of the Russian double-headed eagle and the Chinese dragon covered the bottom of the pool. The tiles were dotted with Martian pennies, good luck wishes from the travelers either coming or going through the bustling arcade.

The walls of the terminal were decorated with murals depicting the settlement of Mars from first touchdown to the present day. As I stood by the pool I looked at scenes of early Russian-Chinese cosmonauts lumbering around in spacesuits beside the prefab huts I had imagined. A later scene showed Burroughs Base as a growing settlement beneath Martian windmills. There were murals depicting the discovery of water beneath ancient sea beds, proof of the wisdom of selecting this site for the first permanent settlement on Mars. Other murals depicted early mining operations, the start of terraforming, the first Martians to be able to take off their spacesuits and breathe the new air of Mars. It was a visual saga of colonization, a testimony to the technologies that were attempting to reshape Mars into the image of Earth.

I looked up. Suspended from the ceiling, like great origami birds, were models of the ever more sophisticated spacecraft that brought settlers to Mars. The first small landers. The great ore freighters. Even the "orphan ships" that brought cheap labor to build the towns and lay the track for the Martian rail system. These reminders of the past floated serenely above me, bathed in my first glimpse of the pink light of Mars that came in hazy abundance through the clerestory windows of the terminal.

I had arrived.

"Bishop?"

I looked down to see a small man with crew cut grey hair and thick goggles standing in front of me. He was as much of a surprise as the lobby had been. I had the romantic notion that Martian settlers would be burly frontier folk, big armed, big chested, square shouldered pioneers who gripped your hand like a vise while they spit on the floor. This man was an owl disguised as a human. His large liquid blue eyes squinted at me through his goggles, magnifying them as if he was looking at me through a microscope.

His face was small and delicate, but weathered by wind and sand. His short frame was covered by rumpled overalls. He had a jazz musician's goatee. When he shook my hand he felt bird-boned beneath the skin. I guessed he was on the far side of middle age, around 70. He smiled expectantly with the imperfect teeth that marked him as one of the Naturals, organic traditionalists who refuse to be sculpted by bio-enhancements.

"Yes I am," I said, trying not to hurt his hand as I shook it.

"I wasn't sure because you don't have your shells on," he said, reaching for my bag. "I'm Oliver Digby. I'm your ride into the city."

"It's very nice to meet you," I said, "but please just call me Tony."

"Bishop Tony," he said happily as we walked toward the exit, "You can just call me Digby."

"Well, thank you, Digby, but you really don't have to carry my bag."

"Oh, I know," he said, "but it's probably a good idea for you to take it easy until you see how your breathing goes. You don't want to over-do it until you get used to the atmosphere."

"I thought Mars was like Earth now," I said hurrying to keep up with him.

"It is," he said over his shoulder, "if you live in the Andes."

Once outside I was bathed in the rosy sky of Mars for the first time. Wisps of thin clouds traced their feathery fingers across a familiar blue, but with a pink glow that dimmed the light and gave the Martian day a subdued sense of an eternal afternoon. Around me a bustle of passengers rolled carts piled with bags either into or out of the terminal. A line of all-terrain vehicles, some canopied, some open aired, jockeyed for parking spaces while black uniformed Mars Central Authority policemen, MACs, whistled them to keep moving.

"Bishop Tony, this is Abba Ambrose."

Climbing out of the vehicle before me, like a stork unfolding itself to fly, was a tall, thin man dressed in grey coveralls. His long legs carried him around the transport in only a few strides and he extended an equally long arm to shake my hand.

"Welcome to Mars, your Grace." His voice intoned the words like a prayer for High Mass.

I shook his hand just as carefully as I had Digby's thinking that all Martians must be birds, their bones seemed so fine.

"Thank you, Abba," I said, "but please just call me Tony."

Looking down from his great height, above an impossibly aquiline nose, Abba Ambrose frowned at the suggestion.

"This way please," he said as he opened the door to the ATV. He sounded like the butler at an English country house. Digby clambered into the rear seat. I took my place on the passenger's side and within a few minutes I was being driven down a wide highway toward my new home on Mars.

We followed Nevsky Prospekt, the main road into the city.

"The nice houses are out here," Digby said from the backseat, "the commercial stuff is closer to the city center."

Being the original settlement, Burroughs Base had grown from a core of the most functional necessities out to the latest luxuries. Like rings of a tree, you can count the years of growth as the city matured. We were on the outer rings, the newest neighborhoods where more affluent Martians can afford to build homes farther from the congested, industrial center. Their houses are brick, locally manufactured Martian brick, and therefore a rusty red color. They are walled, like Spanish style homes, in defense of the sand storms that periodically blow through the city, especially in the Martian winter. Windmills sprout like a forest of metal trees throughout the city. Newer homes have interior gardens, even shallow lily pools, but along with the older homes they all have the most distinctive features of Martian architecture: roof top gardens enclosed in primoglass domes. Old Martian houses look like red boxes wearing "snow-globe" caps. But instead of snow, the globes are a riot of green plants and brightly colored flowers. Before terraforming finally gave Martians a chance to develop outdoor gardens, these greenhouses-on-a-roof were the one source of constant green to which Earth-lonely settlers could retreat. They are still part of the Martian soul, a roof top oasis imbedded in the Martian culture.

Digby pointed to a windmill rising on stilts beside a particularly large house to our right, one of a cluster of houses built in a circle that is the common configuration of Martian suburbs.

"Wind power for home generators," he leaned toward me to make sure I could hear, "you don't really need it anymore since we got the big power station, but most people have one for backup, just in case."

I nodded. Most of the electric power for Mars comes from wind turbines and solar power, although some surprising pockets of geothermal energy have been discovered.

Closer into the city we drove into traffic, more than I had expected. Other ATVs filled the city streets, streets that were growing ever more narrow and winding as we came to the older sections of the town. Residential apartment buildings replaced single homes, a testimony to earlier days when settlers crowded into the boom town. Motorbikes, cheap built Chinese models mixed with a few Russian Harleys, puttered between lumbering transport trucks, daring someone to hit them.

As we came closer we passed warehouses, manufacturing outlets, even an ice skating rink. These larger buildings also had primoglass coverings, but they were rectangular shaped greenhouses.

"Roof farms," said Abba Ambrose, pointing with one long finger, "Early in the settlement every available space was used for agriculture. These mini-farms still supply a wide variety of vegetables, but now they primarily grow delicate plants such as berries or tomatoes."

We continued through narrow avenues into what Ambrose told me was "Old City", the original structures of the town. Most were either temporary housing for the Martian population as it grew or terraform factories when making Mars livable was the priority. These were the

"Water & Air" days for Mars, a generation dedicated to the greening of a dead planet. Thanks to the advanced technologies of Twin Empire scientists, the process took hold and the rest has become Martian history. Over time other settlements were established in different areas of Mars. Some are major agricultural or manufacturing towns, the second stage of development once the terraformers had made life possible without tin suits and oxygen packs. Now there are even some towns that are primarily tourist centers, a third stage that signals the maturity of Martian civilization. Many of these Martian cities and towns are connected by the Martian rapid rail system; the others can be reached by long, over-land drives, but that is across rough terrain and can still be hazardous. Most people prefer using Mars Air.

"Here is the church," said Digby, as we came around a curve, "Looks like a Spanish mission doesn't it?"

It did.

A three language sign out front announced it as "The Barsoom Community Theater". Beneath that was a smaller sign that read "St. Michael and All Angels Common Prayer Church." Like all Common Prayer churches, St. Michael's was primarily a building for public use, but did double duty on Sundays as a place of worship. Its brick walls were covered by Martian stucco, making it the color of a fading rose. It looked like an ancient Spanish mission I had seen once in a holopix, an antique church in a California sunset. Its twin metal doors were painted bright red. A poster on one of the doors said something about a Chekov play, but we were going by too fast for me to read it.

"We are very proud of our community theatre," intoned Abba Ambrose, "perhaps tomorrow you will have an opportunity to see it."

"I will look forward to that," I said.

We drove by the central square of the city, a dusty park with stone pathways and benches, covered by a canopy of green sailcloth. In the center is an original Mars Lander, one of the first to have reached the Red Planet. It is an historic monument to those intrepid days, a memorial to the First Settlers, many of whose families still live on Mars, proudly carrying on the name of Chao, Huan, Valikivosky and Petrof. But now, where the cosmonauts had once scratched out their existence on the hard regolith of Mars, children chase one another under the watchful eyes of Chinese grandparents doing Tai Chi in the park.

One block away we came to Number 13 Yangtze Avenue.

"Well, here we are," said Digby, as the ATV pulled up to the curb. A high wall of plastered brick with a large metal door was all I could see. A faded number 13 was painted by the door.

Digby helped me with my bag again as Ambrose went to unlock the door. The gate swung open with a creak. Inside was an enclosed garden without any plants. An old lawn chair lay on its side as if it had passed out. The metal framework for the house windmill stood in one corner of the garden near a small electric generator. The house itself was the standard Martian brick with clear primoglass windows set into metal frames. Digby tapped the window sills as we walked to the front door up a gravel path.

"Martian steel," he said, "made local."

"I'm afraid it's a little small," Ambrose said flipping on the lights. "It's one of the older houses in this part of town."

I looked into a rectangular room with white plaster walls. An old sofa sagged against one wall. There was a desk, two empty book cases, a Persian style rug that had seen better days and a pole lamp with a Chinese painted shade. The only other decoration in the room was a painting. It hung at an angle in a black metal frame. It looked like Rasputin on a bad hair day.

"What is that?" I asked Digby.

"That is a gift from Saint Michael and All Angels," he said with a smile, "The work of Loreli Quigly, one of your most prominent church members."

"Oh my God," I said without thinking.

"Close," said Digby, "Its Jesus."

Saint Peter was sitting cross-legged in the shade eating olives. I was sitting next to him. Across a path from the olive grove a group of people were gathered in front of a small house.

"Will we see Jesus?" I asked him.

"Soon," said Saint Peter, "Just be patient."

Just then the crowd began to press forward like autograph seekers. A tall man with a beard stepped out.

"Is that him?" I asked jumping to my feet.

"No, I don't know who that is," said Saint Peter.

We waited.

"There he is," said Saint Peter, pointing toward a figure emerging from the crowd. I saw a plump little man with a scraggly beard. His round face looked like a brown moon. His caftan stretched across his belly. It was too long for his diminutive height.

"Wow," I said, "he's not what I expected. He's so...chubby."

"He goes to a lot of dinner parties," said Saint Peter.

"So are you a water prospector?" I asked Digby as we drank Martian tea in my kitchen. I had slept hard my first night on Mars. The sleep of the weary traveler. Digby had returned that morning with a bag of donuts. We were sitting in my galley sized kitchen at a small table. Digby had told me he was a prospector by trade. Having enjoyed my first warm shower at the neighborhood bath house that morning, I wondered if he was a man to thank for it.

"No, not water," he said, "I look for minerals."

"Have any luck finding them?"

"Some," he smiled, "Enough to let me come and go as I please."

"How long have you been at St. Michael's?"

"Oh, I'm not one of your flock," he said through a mouthful of donut, "I don't attend the church. I just help them out when I can. In fact, I help a lot of people when I have the time. You might say I am ecumenical and ubiquitous."

"Ubiquitous," I said, "I like that."

"You'll see," he smiled.

Digby took me for a walk after breakfast. He showed me my neighborhood. We walked past a large apartment building. It had a bland, flat-fronted industrial feeling, a Russian design that was far more functional than aesthetic. There was a noodle shop on the corner just gearing up for the lunch crowd that would come out of the pottery factory at noon. We crossed the road to the city park. The green sailcloth canopy popped gently in the breeze. We stopped to admire the monument to First Settlement. I noticed that the old Lander still bore the markings of the Russian eagle and the Chinese dragon. A plaque gave the date of the historic event.

"They had Mars up and running with air and water," said Digby as we stood in the park, "but it was still pretty crazy when I showed up."

"So were you here in the early days?"

"Oh, yes," he said, "I was just a little boy, but I hit the ground running."

"You weren't born here?"

"No," said Digby, "Orphan ship."

We walked on. I wanted to ask more, but decided not to. I had heard of the orphan ships. After the Drought there were a lot of children left in state run orphanages. Many of them had been transported to Mars as a kind of expendable labor pool. They worked in mines and on desert reclamation projects. It was dangerous work and many died. Not a nice story and I wasn't sure Digby would want to remember it.

We crossed through the park to my local grocery store. Mars is self-sufficient in food. As the atmosphere has grown rich in carbon dioxide, warming enough to allow open air fields, crops have thrived on collective farms that no longer require domes for the hardiest plants. Berries, flowers, and herbs are all still hot housed, but sturdy wheat, barley and root vegetables flourish. They have sustained the Martian diet with a healthy vegetarian menu. A few goats have been imported for milk and cheese, camels for transport, but Martians have evolved a meatless culture.

That seemed to suit my grocer, a cheerful Indian man from one of China's largest provinces, just fine. Digby introduced me as the new Christian bishop when we were checking out. The grocer pointed to a statue of Ganesha, the elephant god, resting on a small shelf behind the counter.

"I am very religious too," he said, "Mars is a very religious place. People of all faiths come here. We even have incense if you need it."

We thanked him and headed home, the grocery bags feeling unnaturally light in my arms, a gift from Martian gravity.

I needed the food because that evening I would host a small dinner for my clergy. The following day, a Sunday, there would be a festive service at the church where I would be welcomed as the new bishop, but first, I would have a quiet dinner with the four priests who were under my care. It was a moment I wanted to get right. If I have learned anything in all of my years in the church it is that next to the Bible, food is the most important thing in Christianity. If you want to gather the flock, you had better be prepared to feed them.

I spent the afternoon cooking. I had bread and a chocolate cake from the local bakery. A mushroom and barley soup simmering on the range that Digby had promised me was a favorite Martian recipe. I was feeling both happy and nervous. I liked the feeling. I liked being in a place I could call home. I liked cooking. For most of my fifty-three years I have lived alone. I am used to feeding myself, but after working in the kitchen with the Sisters at Saint Firetrap's, I have learned the simple joy of feeding others.

I started whistling as I moved around the kitchen. I imagined that my new life was off to a smooth start. I could see no clouds on my horizon. Only Rasputin, glaring at the world from his frame in the living room, seemed to have any doubts about the future.

At dinner that evening, I found out why.

"To hell with that," shouted Ima Maria across the table, "I am not going to bend over and let The Vegas stick it to Mars." She glanced at me, "Pardon my French, bishop, if anybody spoke French anymore."

She was talking to Abba Ambrose who sat opposite her. He and his wife, Felicity, sat motionless but the redness on their cheeks was brighter than the candles on my table. Ima Maria was the priest from Saint Vladimir, a rough mining town 100 kilometers from Burroughs Base. She was a small woman, compact in a trim brown body with black hair, whose Native American features were angled like the Rocky Mountains from which she came. Her eyes flashed when she was angry. Which was often.

"I am as appalled by your language as I am by your opinions," said Abba Ambrose.

If she was a badger of a woman, he was a stork of a man. Long limbed like a scarecrow, his deep set blue eyes peered down the slope of his nose as if they were pools of frozen ice. His face became even more pale and cadaverous as he leaned back from her verbal assault. His voice passed through that great nose with high pitched disdain.

I was about to speak, about to try to calm the storm, when another dinner guest spoke up.

"Got any more wine?" she asked.

I turned to her. She was seated to my right, a large woman with a broad face, an Irish face like mine I thought, with green eyes nestled as if they were sitting in an armchair, relaxed and withdrawn, but weary from the years that had turned her shock of wiry hair grey. The long strands of her unruly hair waved about her head like plumage as she spoke to me. She was Ima Theresa, the priest at Quilong, an artist's colony turned town, up in the hill country near Sharonov where some of the finest pottery on Mars is made for export.

"Never mind," she said with a wry smile, "You've got your hands full. I'll get it."

"I'll help," said my fourth priest, Abba Isidore. He was the youngest of the group, an earnest thirty-something, fresh off the Farm, on his first assignment as the priest of New Shanghai, the wealthiest suburban community on Mars. I imagined he had gotten that plum of a job because he was well connected back home, the son of a prosperous African Free State family, well-educated and well bred, unaccustomed to the bar room brawls of clergy dinners. Or at least, this clergy dinner. He beat a hasty retreat, following Ima Theresa into the kitchen, leaving me alone to referee.

Ima Maria and Abba Ambrose sat at the far end of the table that I had so carefully set up in my living room. The candles I had bought flickered like the tension between them.

"Look," I said, "Let's not get carried away. I understand that you both have strong opinions on this subject. But help me understand. I can't do much to support either one of you if I don't know what is going on."

Maria took a breath and looked at me with an intense expression.

"An invasion of Mars is what is going on," she said, "An invasion from Earth."

"Oh for the love of…" Ambrose began, but Ima Maria raised her voice slightly and continued over him.

"The Vegas is planning to invade Mars," she said, "They want to bring their whorehouses here and set up shop. They are negotiating with Mars Central Authority to open a casino just outside the city. It is going to be called Mega Mars and it will be the ruin of this planet."

I wasn't aware of anything called Mega Mars, but I was aware of what the name implied. In West Hem The Vegas operated many megatainment cities. *Pilgrim's Playground* was built on the site of old Boston. *Everglades* was on the islands left after Florida went underwater. *Amazon Adventure* in the last of the rainforests still clinging to life in Brazil. *Machu Picchu* in Peru. All were theme parks for the sex and gambling industry that kept The Vegas in power. If there was going to be a *Mega Mars* it would follow the same pattern.

"That is a complete exaggeration," said Abba Ambrose, "The Mega Mars project is hardly an invasion. It is development. It will be a carefully restricted, carefully managed entertainment center that will finally bring some culture to this planet."

"Culture?!" shouted Maria, "You call live sex shows culture?"

"They have said there will only be high quality stage shows," said Felicity, "Musicals, theater, even opera." Felicity spoke in a way that always made me think she used the royal "we" when expressing her opinions. She was much shorter than her husband, but no less regal in her presence, a Victoriana of a woman, compact in both features and opinion.

"And you believe that?!" Ima Maria asked sarcastically, "Well, let me sell you some swamp land on Mars."

"Not to mention jobs," said Abba Ambrose pointing that foot-long finger at Maria, "work for potentially thousands of new people who will help to grow this town into a real city."

"Like Pilgrim's Playground?" she yelled, "You call that a city? I call it a whorehouse." She caught herself and looked over at me, "No offense, bishop. I know you are from there."

"None taken," I said, and I was about to say something else when Ima Theresa returned carrying a bottle of wine. Abba Isidore trailed her, holding a pot of coffee in his hands.

"Well, are we having fun yet?" she asked.

"I brought coffee if anyone would like some," he said taking his seat to my left.

"Trust me, stick with the wine," she stage whispered to me, "You're going to need it."

The evening ended after several more volleys between Maria and Ambrose. Isidore did his best to get us off onto talking about the church service the next day, but no one seemed to have the energy to discuss it. Ima Theresa sat in amused silence, watching us over her wine glass. Felicity turned into a statue of cold indifference. Finally, mercifully, we called it a night. I said good-bye to them at the door. I watched them walk down the garden path and out my front gate. Then I closed the door and surveyed the remains of my dinner party. Rasputin glared at me from across the room.

"Whose side are you on?" I asked him as I blew out the candles.

But he didn't say.

The Bishop of Mars

Chapter Three

One week after being officially installed as the Bishop of Mars I found a job. I was happy because it was at the noodle shop on the corner. Jobs on Mars are fairly easy to come by. The economy is expanding. New businesses and corporations are coming to Mars. Old ones are growing. But you have to have the right skills. I am not a miner, farmer, scientist or engineer. So I used my one skill and became a cook. My boss, Mr. Chan, was happy to have me. All of the new immigrants and employees meant more mouths to feed. He was planning to open a second shop across town in the growing suburbs. He needed someone he could trust to run the corner store when he was away, and who better to trust than a noodle making priest?

As for me, I was glad to have both the income and the chance to meet people. All of the clergy in the Common Prayer Church work regular jobs. I learned at the Farm that this wasn't always the case. Once being a priest was like a fulltime job, but after the Drought, all of the Christian denominations collapsed. The idea of a church on every corner fell apart. For religious institutions, it was a question of adapt or die.

The Roman Catholic Church dissolved into three branches. There are three Popes now, just as there once was during the Medieval Age. One remains in Rome, a major trading post for the caravans crossing the salt plains of the Med Marsh from the Sahara; one is in Mandela City, capital of the African Free States; and one is at New Gibraltar where the Atlantic and Pacific have flooded the land that used to connect North and South America.

The Protestant Union is a patch work quilt of storefront churches. They survive, much as we do, with small parishes served by worker clergy. Judaism and Islam are in Diaspora. When the oil ran out and the Sahara swallowed the Middle East, both communities suffered during the chaos that followed. While they lost their nation states, literally to the sands of history, they discovered a new common cause in their shared struggles. Scattered around the Earth and now on Mars, they have become allies in their life as spiritual refugees.

Buddhism, Hinduism, Taoism and Confucianism are flowering in the Chinese Empire. The Russian Orthodox Church, the largest branch of Christianity, does the same in the Russian Empire.

As for us Common Prayer folk, we remain the crazy uncle of organized religion. Quirky to the last. We are traditional like the Orthodox, but out on the street like the Baptizers. We offer support to all three Roman churches and argue just as vehemently with one another as they do. We have a mystical sympathy with Jews and Muslims, but want a sense of order like any good Confucian. We are peace minded like the Buddhists and superstitious like the Taoists. We are, in a word, organic. Like a bowl full of noodles.

So my job suited me. I was dishing out the lunch special when Abba Ambrose turned up unexpectedly, looking slightly out of place in his formal attire as a CPA sitting at the counter next to the pottery workers from the factory next door.

"I would like to have an opportunity to talk," he said, "when you get off work."

"I would be happy to do that," I said, "What if we meet in the park around five? I've been inside all day and I would like to get outside a little before going home."

"Thank you," he said, "Five o'clock in the park." He finished his ramen and left without leaving a tip.

He made up for it though. When he joined me on the park bench he brought a thermos of coffee, an expensive treat. He took one cup from the top and one from the bottom of the thermos, a handy design to make sharing easy since there are no paper products on Mars for use with food or drink. He poured us each a cup and we sat back on the bench, watching some Russian and Chinese kids playing tag.

"I wanted to talk to you about the Mega Mars project," he began, "I did not want you to get the wrong impression."

"I'm listening." I took a sip of coffee. It was really good. Coffee is imported and always a guilty pleasure.

"I know the image we have of The Vegas on Home World," he said, "I am from West Coast and grew up around L.A. Xtreme, the adult theme park. Like you, I have no illusions about the sordid reputation of Vegas megatainment centers. I do not condone them."

"I'm sure you don't," I said, "No priest would."

Ambrose looked out at the children running past us beneath the green sailcloth canopy.

"I would not want to bring that kind of degradation to Mars," he said, "But this situation is different. Mars is different. We are still a frontier. A community that is rough around the edges." He looked at me, "I don't need to tell you that we already have our fair share of bars and brothels. It is not like we are an innocent utopia."

I nodded. I had seen the bars and strip joints on the drive into Burroughs Base. They were where many of the local miners, factory workers and construction crews went to let off steam on a Saturday night.

"The point is, we don't have an alternative. We don't have refinement."

"What about your community theatre at St. Mike's?" I asked, "You did a pretty good job with Chekov."

Abba Ambrose snorted through his nose, "Oh yes, an amateur theater for Shakespeare in overalls". He leaned toward me and out came that finger again, stabbing the thin Martian air between us, "What I am talking about is the arts. The real arts. The classical arts. The Mega Mars project promises to bring those to Mars. Legitimate theater with some of the best actors. Ballet from Saint Petersburg. Chinese opera. The Moscow Symphony."

"And you believe those promises?"

"The government believes them," he said sharply, "They have said that the Mega Mars complex will be strictly regulated and supervised."

I took a long drink of coffee. I looked over at Abba Ambrose. His stork like body bent toward me as taut as the wires holding up the sailcloth above our heads.

"Listen, Abba," I said at last, "I know that you and Ima Maria see things very differently on this subject…"

"Oh that woman is impossible," he said almost spilling his coffee. I held up one hand.

"Please, let me finish. I know that you each have strong opinions. She comes from West Hem too. I respect her views because I have seen how much anyone can rely on promises from The Vegas…"

He started to interrupt.

"…but…but," I said, "I hear what you are saying. Mars is a different reality. It would be the first time The Vegas would be permitted to open one of their centers within the borders of the Empires. That could make a difference."

"I only ask that you keep an open mind," he said.

"I understand."

"Don't be swayed by…by emotional arguments."

"I understand."

"And consider the economic benefits," he said, "The Mega Mars project promises to create hundreds of new jobs."

As the pink light of the Martian afternoon turned to lavender, we said our good-byes and I walked home. I had promised to keep an open mind. I had promised to look into it more thoroughly before I took a position as the bishop of Mars. But what worried me was that word, promise. There seemed to be a lot of promises being made. I knew I would keep mine. I wasn't so sure about The Vegas.

I had two ComCom calls when I got home. I was standing in my living room having a staring contest with Rasputin when the first one came in. It was from Ima Theresa .

"I just want to make sure that we are all set for your official visit," she said.

"That's two weeks from next Sunday?"

"Right," she said, "I have five baptisms and eighteen confirmations."

"I'll be there Saturday night," I replied, "I'm coming in on the 4 o'clock Air Mars flight. I made reservations. We can have dinner and talk. I'm really looking forward to it."

"I'll pick you up at the airport," she said, "See you in two weeks."

That brief conversation sort of sums up my job as a bishop. The word for bishop in ancient Greek, *episcope*, means overseer. That's what I do. As the bishop, I make my rounds to see how things are going. I visit each congregation. Back on Home World, where there may be many congregations in a bishop's territory, a diocese, that can take some time. In a tiny pioneer diocese like Mars, things are on a much more intimate scale. We have only four congregations with priests, although we hope to establish more. The confirmations Ima Theresa mentioned are among my special duties as a bishop. When a person decides that he or she wants to join the Common Prayer Church, a bishop lays hands on them to confirm them into that decision. In effect, she was telling me that she had eighteen new people who wanted to join our church. It was a sign that although small, our little diocese was healthy and growing.

The second call I received that night was long distance from Earth.

It was from Clare. While face-to-face calls between Earth and Mars are possible on the ComCom they are expensive. Clare sent me a holopix pre-pack, a recorded message. I sat on the sofa and watched her face appear before me on my ComCom.

"I hope you are getting your Mars legs by now," she said smiling, "They tell me it takes a while to get used to the gravity. I have the image of you bouncing around like a rabbit. Things here are fairly quiet. There have been a few more grumbles about my appointing you as the missionary bishop for Mars, but nothing outrageous. They say it was nepotism on my part and that I should have picked an older, more experienced priest. I just remind them that you are almost middle-aged and Mars needs a young fifty-something bishop to keep up with the frontier boom-town. That gets them off into fuming about how I got to be Archbishop in the first place and we go around the circle again. But that's just the dance I always have to do with the conservatives. The church at large is very excited about what you are doing. Our first diocese on another planet! I guess you know you are in the history books now. I guess we both are. Who would have imagined that back at Saint Firetrap's? Me, the head of the church. You, the first bishop on Mars. Amazing. There's got to be some proof of God in there somewhere, don't you think? Or at least, of God's mystical sense of humor. Anyway, I just wanted to say hello and tell you I am praying for you. Clarence too. Both of us are praying for you. Keep us posted on how it is going. The Sisters all send their love. They are mailing you a scarf Sister Margaret knitted for you. They are afraid you will get cold up there. How cold is it anyway? I better not run this bill up. They charge by the minute I think. Just take good care of everybody. Yourself too. We are all very proud of you, Lucky. Bye for now and God bless you."

I played the message over three times. I sat on the sofa, looking at Clare's face mouthing the words from what seemed a lifetime away. It made me feel homesick. I decided to get busy so I wouldn't think about

Earth. I went into the kitchen and climbed the metal corkscrew stairs to the roof garden.

My dome was a mess, just empty metal shelves with a few containers where plants should be. Digby had promised to help me get it organized when he returned from one of his frequent disappearing acts, the coming and going that made him in his own word, ubiquitous. But even in its messy state, I loved sitting in my roof top garden. Older Martian houses are just brick boxes with a few windows, built to give shelter from sand storms. The garden actually serves the purpose of holding the bricks in place, a weight to compress the bricks and make the whole structure sound. And yet, the function is a blessing in disguise. The garden is a bubble of clear primoglass, an open window to the sky. It has a sensor at the top that can drop a canopy over the dome to protect it from abrasion in the worst of the sand storms, but it is usually an open space, full of light, either the soft pink daylight of Mars, or the light of Martian night when the twin moons, Phobos and Deimos, race across the sky in an eternal game of celestial tag.

I sat on a crate and took out the holopix of Clare. I thumbed it on and placed it on a shelf before me. The yellow lights of the city sparkled in the cold Martian night around me. I started cleaning up the clutter of my garden. I swept up the dirt. I hung up the few gardening tools. I left the holopix on as if Clare were there in the garden with me, watching me get my life organized. She was watching over me.

Episcope.

I kept watch over Mars. Clare kept watch over me.

Working alone in my garden that night I had the feeling someone else was keeping watch over us both.

The Virgin Mary was knitting a scarf. She was sitting on a crate.
"Who is that for?" I asked.
"For Clare," she said, "She needs it to stay warm. Two-Fers get

colder than other people."

"Really?" I said, "I didn't know that."

"Oh yes," said Mary, "It's a proven fact. They get twice as cold."
She held up the scarf. It was blue.

"I wonder why?" I asked.

She put the scarf down and looked at me.

*"That's a good question," she said, "Maybe it has something to
do with the fact that they have more people inside them than we do."*

"Twice as many chances to get cold," I smiled.

*"Or three," said Mary taking up her knitting again, "I can't tell
you how many scarves I have made for my son."*

On Saturday I decided to borrow Digby's ATV and get out of the
city. The pottery factory was closed so Mr. Chan didn't need me at the
noodle shop. Digby had left his old ATV parked at my place. I had no
idea where he went, but we had a standing agreement that I could use
it whenever I wanted. I just had to put in the fuel.

I drove to an oxymeth station. Out front was a sign that showed a
little green man wearing a hat with the logo for Mars Fuel on it.
Digby's ATV, like all ground transport on Mars, runs on methane-
oxygen diluted with carbon dioxide. It is a renewable fuel that is easy
to refine on Mars and has the added benefit of producing water as a
by-product. A container on the back of the ATV captures the water to
be recycled later into making more fuel.

Martian ATVs come in three basic models, the cheap open air steel
frame and independent suspension rattle box that Digby drives; an
enclosed two door version with a canopy to keep the wind and sand
out of your face; and a luxury model with four doors and climate
control. The St. Vladimir steel plant also turns out a Martian pickup
and large truck. All of these vehicles have four wheel drive, a necessity
on the rough off-road terrain of Mars. I fueled up and drove out the

Nevsky Prospekt heading away from town.

I followed the tarmac leading out of the city toward the west, toward the highlands that were once the shore line of a Martian sea. I had no particular plan in mind, but I knew that the Mega Mars Project was scheduled to be built out there and I wanted to see it. Not that there would be much to see. The flatlands of Mars are an iron oxide desert littered with rocks. They can go on for many unbroken kilometers, until suddenly there is a break in the land, either great mountains pushed up or deep canyons scoured down.

I bounced along at a slow pace. The tarmac ends at the methane refinery on the far edge of Burroughs Base. After that, it is open country.

I figured that as long as I kept going west I would eventually run into the future construction site. The Vegas planned to extend the tarmac out to the Mega Mars complex, so I knew if I kept going straight I would have to find it.

And find it I did. I came over a small hill and in the distance I saw something so odd that it made me stop. It was a large billboard. Out in the middle of the desert, standing on two metal legs sunk deep into the Martian regolith, The Vegas had constructed a billboard announcing the future home of Mega Mars. It was their way of showing that they could dominate anything, even the Martian desert. Back on Home World, Vegas projects were intentionally built in places where the natural beauty of the land could be overlaid with chrome and plastic. *Amazon Adventure, Machuu Pichuu, Denali Dome*, they all were incongruous architectural fantasies forced onto the landscape by the sheer brute force of Vegas engineering. This billboard was not on the scale of a casino sitting on top of Inca ruins or a strip club beneath the last trees of the Amazon forest, but it was a hint of things to come.

I drove up to the billboard and got out. A breeze ruffled the sand. I looked up at the sign.

I have heard it said that religion gives people mixed messages. You are loved by a caring God, but if you screw up you will go to hell for eternity. That kind of thing. But the church is not the only purveyor of mixed messages. On The Vegas billboard was a near-naked woman gesturing with her hand toward a cornucopia of classical culture. The stripper was introducing Mars to ballet dancers, a symphony orchestra, Chinese opera performers, and a host of famous actors dressed in costume. The woman was a showgirl, complete with a plumed headdress. Her breasts were exposed to the Martian sky. With the graceful sweep of her hand she was showing Mars what The Vegas intended to bring to the desert.

Behind the cornucopia was a stylized version of what Mega Mars would look like. It was a giant dome, larger than anything ever constructed on the planet. Beneath the dome was the casino and theater complex. Miniature people were walking up winding ramps to take in the show. Mega Mars was presented as a glittering Oz of entertainments and fun.

COMING SOON. MEGA MARS. A TREASURE OF CULTURE FOR THE RED PLANET.

I looked around. The open desert was a table top of orange-brown sand sprinkled with thousands of rocks. In the distance a small dust devil whirled across the surface beneath the pink light of afternoon.

I looked back at the showgirl. She was staring toward the horizon, her face frozen in a permanent red lipped smile. *COMING SOON.*

I walked back to the ATV. I sat looking up at the billboard in the empty desert. A passage from the Hemish Bible flickered through my mind.

What did you go out into the wilderness to see?

It was a question Jesus asked his followers about John the Baptist, the prophet who railed against the corruption and greed of his time. What had they expected to see and hear from John? What had they expected to find?

What had I expected to find out here? A sign of something I

already knew?

The garish billboard was certainly a sign. It was classic Vegas. An assault on Nature. A demonstration of power. A mixed message. A seduction.

What did you go out into the wilderness to see?

I started Digby's old ATV and turned around. I began the slow, bumpy drive back to Burroughs Base. The afternoon sun was hanging low in the sky. There should be plenty of light to get me home, I thought. No rush. I did not want to break an axel by trying to drive too fast over the rocks.

As I bounced along the desert floor I remembered a lifetime of images like the ones on the sign. Pilgrim's Playground is awash in them. Wall sized advertisements for the casinos. Messages played on holosigns by the roadways, in the transit shuttles, even floating in the air above the streets. Happy gamblers. Contented drunks. Cheerful anonymous sex. I had grown up in a world where these messages are an endless visual reality. They had not made me prudish. I felt no deep sense of moral outrage. They just were. And they were everywhere.

West Hem is the land of the mixed message. Grow old but look young. Be rich but have nothing. Waste life and life will be fun. What had I come out into the Martian desert to see that I had not already seen a million times before?

Nothing. Except that it was here, in a place it had never been before.

It was not the message that disturbed me. It was the location. The billboard was like a melanoma. The first faint sign of something growing on the skin. On the superheated Earth, melanomas are one of the leading causes of death among the poor. The Vegas is like one giant melanoma spreading on Home World. Now the first sign, literally, of it appeared here, on the clean desert of Mars.

Ima Maria was right. Earth is invading Mars. One promise at a time.

Earth is invading Mars, that is exactly what I was thinking when I drove into a sand trap. I had been distracted. I had my mind on the billboard, on The Vegas, on Ima Maria, letting the monotone scenery of the desert lull me into driving on mental autopilot. Big mistake. I drove into a Transverse Aeolian Ridge. That's the fancy name for sand trap on Mars. There is nothing quite like them on Earth. Even in the Sahara they do not exist. They only appear on Mars where the consistency of the sand and the wind patterns create a series of ridges, like rows of icing squirted out of a baker's decorating bag. Only these serpentine lines are made of sand as fine as flour. An ATV can lose traction, get beached on underlying rock, and spin its wheels with no hope of recovery.

That's just what happened to me. Digby's old ATV wallowed helplessly in the sand. I gunned the engine. A typical reaction with typical results. The ATV just settled in deeper. I sat in the driver's seat for a few moments letting the reality sink in. I had the "this-can't-be-happening-to-me" feeling. But it was happening. I got out of the ATV. I decided I might be able to rock the carriage loose. Or pull it loose.

I tried rocking the ATV as violently as I could. It seemed to lean at an angle, sliding deeper into the sand on one side. I climbed back in and revved the motor. I only kicked up more sand.

I swore and got out again. I looked around as if expecting help to appear just because I needed it. All I saw was the sun dropping lower toward the horizon.

I decided to pull the ATV forward, hoping to dislodge it from any rocks beneath it. I went around to the front. My knees were buried in the floury sand. I grabbed the frame and gave an experimental pull. Even though Digby's machine is an open air model, it is still heavy, too heavy to be moved with a tug.

I felt for a better footing under the sand. My left foot found a rock and I tried to brace myself on it for a good yank. I took a breath and pulled forward with one strong pull.

My foot slipped. I felt a white hot pain shoot through my ankle and I went down into the sand.

I swore as tears filled my eyes. I had not moved the ATV an inch. I had only twisted my ankle.

I sat in the sand breathing heavily. My ankle was pulsing a message of pain into my brain. I suddenly felt cold. I looked at the ATV. I cursed again. I made myself try to stand. My left ankle put an electric current through my leg. I grabbed at it and sat back down.

Now what?

The lengthening shadows of the dying day seemed to send out dark purple fingers into the sand trap. I was still several kilometers away from Burroughs Base. The chances of someone driving out in my direction were next to nothing. I fumbled in my overalls looking for my handheld ComCom. I could call for help.

Nothing.

I had left it on the kitchen table. I could see it sitting there in my mind. Like an idiot, I had left it behind. I had hurried out of the house, excited to be going out into the desert for the first time. Now, maybe the last time.

Night was coming. Although Mars has warmed considerably, it still gets frigid at night. Too cold to be sitting outside with a busted ankle. I was wearing overalls but I had no thermal gear. If I did not get help I could die of exposure.

I stood up again, accepting the pain. I shuffled my way out of the sand and tried a few tentative hops forward. The low gravity of Mars made me miscalculate and I came down in a crunch of hurt onto the desert floor. I lifted myself up. I half hopped, half hobbled forward. I made it out of the sand and found solid ground.

At least I could crawl.

And I did crawl. I felt the rough surface of the Martian regolith scour my hands. The light was fading quickly. The cold was creeping up my back. I could see nothing before me but more sand and more rock. The pain in my left leg was getting worse. I wondered if I was going into shock. I tried not to imagine what I looked like. Seeing myself crawling on my stomach into the night only made the fear grow stronger. I was having trouble breathing in the thin Martian air. Hyperventilating.

I have been in dangerous places before, but they were always familiar places. Stairways and alleyways. City streets and transit tunnels. But never outside in a place like this. Never in an empty world. As the stars filled the sky that emptiness swallowed me. I could not see the ground before me. I began to shiver. Blindly, I pulled myself over and around rocks, cutting my hands. Where was I going anyway? I had no idea. Out. Away. Anywhere. I was just moving along the track of pain, willing myself to keep moving.

Finally my hand slipped on a large rock and I fell forward against it, scraping the side of my face. I lay on the icy desert floor, breathing. Just breathing. That was about all I had left. Breathing fast. Breathing shallow. Breathing against the cold and the numbness.

I closed my eyes. I could see my small ComCom sitting on the kitchen table. Too bad he left it. What an idiot. Went out into the desert alone. Didn't tell anyone where he was going. Drove into a sand trap. What an idiot.

What did he go out into the wilderness to see?

No one would ever know.

Chapter Four

Mary Magdalene was floating over me. She was wearing a headscarf. Her eyes were like almonds.

"Where am I?" I asked her.

"You've been in an accident," she said in Russian, "We are taking you to hospital."

"I didn't know you were Russian," I said.

"Aren't you?" she asked.

"Where's Jesus?"

"I don't know," she said.

"Can I ask you something?"

"Of course," she said. Her voice was very soft and kind, but far away.

"Are you married?"

Mary Magdalene gave me a strange smile.

"No," she said, "I am single."

"So the stories aren't true?" I said.

"What stories?" she asked.

"That you and Jesus are married."

Mary Magdalene laughed.

"No, that's not possible." She said.

"Why?"

"Because I'm a Muslim."

"Wow, really? That's a lot different than what most people say

about you."

"What do they say about me?"

Digby was sitting in a metal chair next to my bed. Pink sunlight was coming through the windows. I could hear voices in the hallway.

"So have a lot of people heard what happened to me?" I asked.

Digby nodded, "Almost everyone on the planet. Mars is a small town. People like to talk. You are a newcomer with a public job. You almost killed yourself and only got saved thanks to a mysterious and beautiful young woman. Yeah, I'd say the story has made the rounds."

I looked at the baskets of mushrooms that crowded the windowsills and table tops of my room. They were get well mushroom baskets. Mushrooms grow very well on Mars and have become a staple of the Martian diet. Before there were flowers, there were mushrooms. Martians continue to use them in the same way as people on Home World use bouquets of flowers.

"Do they think I'm a moron?"

Digby shuffled in his chair.

"Well, they wonder why you drove off into the desert without telling anyone where you were going," he said.

I moaned and not from pain.

"They wondered why you didn't have any survival gear with you and why you thought you could pull an ATV out of a sand trap."

I moaned again.

"But most of all, they wondered why you didn't have your ComCom on you."

I groaned out loud.

"So they think I am a moron."

"Pretty much," said Digby brightly, "It was a classic greenhorn thing to do and you did it up big."

"I am sorry about the ATV," I said, looking over at him.

"We got a tow truck and pulled it out," he said, "You can't really hurt that old jalopy."

We sat in silence for a moment. Digby reached over and popped a mushroom in his mouth.

"When did you get back?" I asked him. Digby had been off on one of his mysterious rambles around Mars. I had not seen him until I woke up in the hospital in Burroughs Base.

"Just about the time the Muslim girl brought you in," he said, "They called your ComCom from the hospital to see if you had any family. It was on your kitchen table. I picked it up and then came right over to the ER."

"It was a miracle she found me," I said looking down at my bandaged ankle.

"No doubt about it," he said standing up to stretch. His small frame was still in dirty overalls. His oversized goggles rested on his head like tiny antlers. "Only madmen and Muslims go out in the Martian night," he said.

"What's that?"

"Oh, just a scrap of an old saying. Muslims are a very religious people on Mars," he said, "Very devout people. Very spiritual. Sometimes they go out into the desert to fast and pray."

"Is that what she was doing?" I asked.

Digby nodded again, "Apparently. She was coming in to town after being out for a long stretch. Wanted to buy some supplies to take back to her people at their settlement over at New Medina. She stumbled across you, wrapped you up, and called for an emergency truck. She rode in with you and got you into the hospital before she took off again."

"She must think I am a moron," I said, "I never even got to tell her thank you for saving my life."

Digby walked over to the bed and looked down at me with his owl eyes.

"I don't think *moron* is the word for it," he said smiling at me, "*crazy* is the word she used. She said that you were pumped up with pain killers and kept asking her if she was married. You thought she was married to Jesus and when she said no you proposed to her. Something about making an honest woman out of her. I'm not sure if she took it the right way. I think you offended her."

I closed my eyes and groaned.

"Oh my God," I said on my bed of pain, "Please just leave me here to die."

"Sure," said Digby patting my arm, "Can I take some mushrooms before I go?"

Digby, true friend as ever and a man of constant surprises, was covering for me at the noodle shop while I rested up at home. I was sitting in my living room when I got a call from Ima Maria. I had gotten calls and messages from all the clergy and from some people I did not even know. It made me feel a little better in one way, but a lot worse in another way. I hated having to retell my story because it only reminded me of what a moron I had been.

"So what were you doing out there?" Ima Maria asked. Her face was hovering over my holopix pad. I sat on the sofa with my leg propped up, a cup of Martian tea in my hand.

"Nothing," I said, "I just went for a drive."

"Uh huh," she said dubiously, "Some drive."

"Let's talk about something else," I suggested.

"Sure... so when is the wedding?"

"Oh, for God's sake. Don't tell me you have heard that story over in Saint Vlad too?"

She laughed, "Are you kidding? Everyone has heard it. Mars is a small town, bishop. I'm afraid news travels fast. You and Mary Magdalene out in the desert. You wanting to make an honest woman out of her. And she turns out to be one of the most serious minded Muslim women on Mars. Who could make up a story like that?"

"Well please don't help it along, ok? I don't think the lady would appreciate it and I sure don't."

"Ok, I'm sorry," she said quickly, "I didn't mean to hit a sore spot. It's just so funny if you know her."

"Do you know her?" I asked sitting up.

"A little," said Ima Maria, "I've met her. Very nice looking woman. Very serious. She's a teacher out at New Medina. Very religious. Just your type."

I started to tell her to stop with the jokes, but was too curious.

"So what is her name?" I asked.

"They didn't tell you?" asked Maria. I shook my head. "Alima," she said, "Alima Shariff."

"Oh," I said, absently, "Alima Shariff."

"Better be careful," said Maria, "You wouldn't want to make Jesus jealous."

I glared into the holopix. She raised both hands in surrender.

"Sorry," she said, "Honestly. Let me tell you the other reason I called."

She went on to tell me that she was having a town meeting at the union hall that served as her parish church. Saint Vladimir is an industrial town. Steel works. ATV manufacture. Irrigation pumps and tubing. Any of the heavier industries. It is a blue collar town, a place where men and women work long hours with their hands and are proud of it. Ima Maria's church, Saint Peter's, is their all-purpose community center. It is part union hall, part health clinic, part adult education center. On Sundays the steelworkers and truck builders crowd in to worship with the priest they have come to adopt as their own, the small woman with the fiery temper, as hot as the furnaces at Mars Steel.

"We've got to do something to stop this Mega Mars project before the government signs on the dotted line," she said, "We have to get organized."

"I'm afraid I can't be there for the meeting," I said, "I'm booked to go to Quilong next Sunday."

"I know," she said, "that's ok. I just wanted you to know that I am hosting a meeting about it."

"What do you plan to do?"

"I don't know yet," she frowned, "but time is running out. The Vegas lawyers are coming to Mars to seal the deal. We have to take some action before they get here."

"When are they coming?"

"Snake Month," she said, "around 30 Snake."

I shifted my brain into overdrive to make sense out of what she had just said. The Martian calendar is different from that on Home World. Mars has a year with 669 days. These days are longer than their Earth counterparts. Trying to parse them out into more equal months is not easy because the Martian orbit is elliptical. To create a twelve month calendar, a Martian month is calculated as 30 degrees of travel around the Sun. So there are twelve Martian months, from 47 to 65 days long. They are named after the signs of the Chinese zodiac. Maria was talking to me at the end of Horse Month, the last of the Martian summer.

"I'm sorry," I said, "It is going to take me a while to get the calendar straight in my head."

"No problem," she said, "The point is, The Vegas wants to wrap up the negotiations before the sand storm season in Dragon Month. That means we have to get organized and put pressure on the government before they get here."

"What kind of pressure?" I asked feeling a little anxious.

"A protest of some kind," she said, "Direct action."

I took a gulp of tea. My ankle suddenly started to ache.

"Look," I said, "I would rather bring this up before the whole church at our diocesan convention."

Ima Maria gave me a dubious look.

"I don't think passing a resolution at convention is going to make a lot of impact," she said slowly.

"Maybe not," I agreed, "but it does give all of the representatives from the four churches a chance to come together to take a unified position."

"It could be a waste of time," she said with a frown, "Abba Ambrose and his conservative friends are not going to go along with any resolution to condemn The Vegas plan."

"They could change their minds if we had a persuasive case to argue," I said. I could see she wasn't convinced. "Listen, why don't you have your town hall meeting and gather the opinions of your community. I am going to hobble over to Quilong this weekend on Mars Air and I will see what they think. We can compare notes when I get back."

Ima Maria took a deep breath.

"You're the bishop," she said, "I will do what you think best, but I am still not convinced that we don't need to take this issue to the streets."

"One step at a time, Maria," I said, "I understand how you feel. I don't like The Vegas project any more than you do, but if we are going to challenge it, we have a lot of spadework to do."

She didn't speak for a moment. Then she looked at me.

"One last question…"

"Sure," I said, "What is it?"

"Can I be a bridesmaid?"

"Oh, for God's sake."

I was drifting off the surface of Mars. Slowly, majestically, I was rising above Burroughs Base.

I could see the top of the Roman arches that formed the roof of the spaceport terminal. The green moss that covered it reminded me of Digby's crew cut. I could see the straight line of the Nevsky Prospekt leading into the city with a stream of ATVs and trucks moving along it like toys. As I rose higher, I saw the whole spread of the city, windmills like whirligigs spinning above domes filled with flowers. Rows of Martian houses were nestled behind their courtyard walls. The apartment houses were brick boxes with rectangles of glass reflecting the pink light of the day like prisms. Streamers of steam, vented from the factories, waved like ghostly fingers in the thin Martian breeze. In the distance, the methane refinery poked metal tubes into the soft underside of the milky-rose sky. I saw all of these things as I floated in silence, only the faint hum of the motors behind me droning my mind to sleep.

"First time in a dirigible?" the man beside me asked.

I turned to look at him. We were standing on the observation deck of Mars Air flight 27, the regular run from Burroughs Base to Quilong. Its logo, a familiar advertising motif on Mars, showed a little green man wearing an antique flight cap with goggles.

"Yes, first time" I said, "I've never been in a blimp before."

He smiled at me. He was a middle aged European dressed in clean overalls and holding an expensive looking travel bag.

"Blimp, dirigible, zeppelin," he said looking down at the city, "a rose by any other name, but always a delight. My favorite way to travel."

"It's so quiet," I said.

"Peaceful," he replied, "Like floating in a bubble."

We stood for a while watching the city drift behind us. The desert floor soon became the only scenery. The regolith of Mars stretched out like an orange rug, wrinkled as if it were sitting on a hardwood floor without a mat to hold it taut. Small hills bunched it into ripples. The endless sprinkling of stones dotted the surface as though someone had spilled marbles on the rug, a careless coating of rocks as far as the eye could see.

A Mars Air flight attendant came through the cabin with a tray of green tea. I took a cup and sat in a lounge chair, resting my crutches next to me. The man joined me, placing his bag on the floor and his tea cup on a small table between us.

"Don't tell me," he said with a broad smile, "I bet you are the Bishop of Mars."

"Well, yes I am. How did you know? Are you a member of one of our churches?"

"No, no," he laughed cheerfully, then looking at my bandaged ankle he said, "I've heard about how the new bishop wandered off into the desert and hurt his ankle. I know there is a Common Prayer parish in Quilong. I just put two and two together."

I sunk a little deeper into my chair. I wondered how much more of the story he had heard. I took a drink of tea.

"I imagine this will be your first visit to Quilong," he said, mercifully changing the subject.

I nodded, sipping my tea.

"You'll love it," he said, "One of the most beautiful places on Mars. It's an artist's colony, you know."

"Yes, I've heard that."

"Spectacular scenery," he continued, "Up in the hill country. Nothing like a sunset in Quilong. Wait till you see it."

"I understand they make pottery there."

"Oh, absolutely. Wonderful pottery. In fact, that's my business. I am an art dealer. I export Quilong pottery and ceramics to Home World."

We spent much of the rest of the flight talking. His name was Duvalier. He was from the Euro province of the Russian Empire, but he exported Martian art to both Russia and China. Even some to West Hem, although he felt the nouveau riche magnates of The Vegas who bought it had no real appreciation for it other than its cost. The Chinese were the real connoisseurs, he told me, for they had a deep sensitivity to the true art of the glaze and enamel work that could transform simple red clay into a thing of beauty.

By the time the dirigible was gliding toward the hills of Quilong I had learned how this once small outpost of Martian eccentrics had become a thriving town of both fine artists and artisans. It supported itself by manufacturing sturdy earthenware for daily use throughout Mars and by producing delicate pottery and ceramics for people like Mr. Duvalier. There was even a small but growing tourist business with bed and breakfast accommodations for the sightseeing traveler. It was this last bit of information that should have prepared me for the first person I met as I hobbled off my flight.

"Rabbi, what a surprise to see you again!" she said. It was Esther Kaminski.

"Well, hello," I said, propping myself on my crutches to shake her hand.

"Oh my goodness," she said looking down at my ankle, "so it's true. I heard that you had hurt yourself in a sand trap. I plan to warn people about those in my book."

"Just an accident," I said quickly, "I'll be fine."

"Oh, but that's too bad. You won't get to do any rock climbing while you are here."

"Ah, no," I said, "Is there rock climbing in Quilong?"

"It's one of the unexpected treasures of Quilong. Most people come for the pottery and the sunsets. But I will introduce them to the added bonuses of rock climbing and mud baths."

"So the book is going well?"

"It's writing itself," she said happily.

"That's great. It is good to see you again."

"You too," she said, "Now I am going to experience the night flight to Burroughs Base, another must do for the traveler who wants to see the true beauty of Mars."

We said our good-byes. I watched her walk away. Not for the first time in my life I marveled at the truly happy person. Esther Kaminski seemed to like who she was and what she did. What a rare gift, I thought. How few people seem to be born at peace with themselves.

"Hi," a voice spoke behind me, "You must be bishop Tony."

I turned to look into another face that seemed happy with its life. He was a twenty-something Chinese man with his long silky hair tied up into a knot on a beautifully shaped head, the kind of head I imagined artists like to draw. His eyes were chocolate brown and warm beneath long lashes. No doubt about it, this young man could be a model for any Martian Michelangelo.

"Yes, I am," I said.

"I could tell by the crutches," he smiled, "They said you had got stuck in a sand trap and hurt yourself."

"Oh, it was nothing really," I said quickly, and then to change the subject, "You must be my ride to town?"

"Billy Wu," he said, "Senior Warden. Ima Theresa had to work late, so I volunteered to be your taxi."

He gave me a small bow. I returned it. Senior Wardens are the head of the vestry, the committee that runs any Common Prayer Church. In effect, the laity, the people in the pews, are the real authority in the church. While clergy types like me carry out the sacramental duties, the laity do almost everything else. They build the churches, keep them running, raise the money and decide how to spend it. They take their part in every worship service. They are the church. Without them, I would be bishop of nothing. Billy deserved the bow.

"My uncle is your neighbor, you know, Dr. Wu Zhaohui," he said as we walked out of the Quilong airport, "You may not have met him yet. He's been out in the field for over a month. Way down in the Valles Marineris."

The Valles Marineris is one of the wonders of Mars: a canyon four times the size of the Grand Canyon.

"Lucky guy," I said, "Is he a scientist?"

"Terraformer," said Billy, "The most famous on Mars."

We climbed into Billy's pick up. The truck bed was full of tools, bags of clay, and wire. Billy started it up and we drove away from the small brick building with a windsock that served Quilong as its airport.

"How about you?" I asked, glancing back at the equipment that rattled around behind us, "Are you a terraformer too?"

He laughed. "No, I'm a potter."

"Well, in some ways that doesn't make you so different from you uncle."

"How's that?" asked Billy.

"You both are into transforming the clay on Mars."

"Never thought of it that way," he said, slowing down for a small boy leading a goat down the dirt road to Quilong, "Must run in the family."

We drove the two kilometers from the airport to the town as Billy pointed out the landmarks. The tiny airport sits on top of a mesa, flat land with no updrafts, ideal for the dirigible service that runs year round, except for sand storm season. The town itself is over and down the lip of the mesa, huddled alongside rippled cliffs of exposed Martian regolith. As we came to the edge of the mesa I got my first panoramic view of what will make Quilong such an important chapter in Esther Kaminski's book.

Quilong looks down on the vast open expanse of the Chryse Planitia, open desert that is the archetype of unbroken beauty on Mars. To the west, it looks up to the vast formation of the Sharonov Crater, a monumental cone of deep red Martian crust standing as high as a mountain. A wall of sharp ridges and orange hills topped by a mountain of breathtaking beauty on one side, and an endless plain of violet shadowed grandeur on the other: Quilong is a crossroads for the best that Mars has to offer to any soul not stillborn to the mystery of creation.

"It's incredible," I said quietly as we curved down the steep road into the town.

"Once you've seen it, it's a hard place to leave," said Billy.

He pulled onto a scenic overlook so we could watch the afternoon sun. There were several other ATVs parked there for the same reason.

"But here's the best part," he said, "Watch."

The sun seemed to roll down the side of the distant mountain-crater, like a glowing pink ball. As it did so, its rays touched the edges of the jagged cliffs and suddenly they began to sparkle. First, only in glimmers. A twinkle of crystal here, another there, but then, like a swarm of fireflies gathering in shadows, the whole face of the cliffs around Quilong came alive in a dance of light. It was, in a word, breathtaking.

"I have never seen anything so beautiful," I said.

"God is a first class potter," said Billy quietly, "No one can create a glaze like that who isn't an artist."

We watched the light show for several more minutes then drove silently into the town. It was hard to see in the gathering dark, but Quilong is a mountain town, a series of adobe style huts clustered in and around the cliffs. Its quaint streets are winding trails through what I imagined Esther would call a fairy village on Mars, a Munchkin town of round houses and conical roofs. Because a wind farm on the mesa top supplies energy, there are no windmills in Quilong itself, but there are revolving solar antennas that catch the morning sun to power the kilns that seem to stand beside most of the houses.

"Ima Theresa will be off work soon," said Billy as we drove up to a large geodesic dome perched on a solid outcropping of rock, "This is her place. You can make yourself at home till she gets back."

He helped me get my bag into the dome. A small kitchen area was separated from the rest of the interior by a long table and mismatched chairs. The floor was a patchwork quilt of many colored Turkish and Chinese rugs. Two old sofas and a couple of comfortable stuffed chairs formed a place for relaxation and talk around a central hearth of electrically heated Martian fire-rocks, stones that captured and held heat on cold winter nights. Curtains suspended on wires created sleeping alcoves with hammocks for beds.

Billy and I said good-byes as I thanked him for the ride and told him I would look forward to meeting his uncle one day soon.

"He's a trip," said Billy smiling, "A regular mystic."

Then he left me sitting on a sofa with a glass of iced tea in my hand. I propped my leg up on a small ottoman. It ached after the trip, but I had been too engaged in everything I had experienced and seen that day to notice. The dirigible ride. The beauty of Quilong. It couldn't get much better than this I was thinking when the door opened and Ima Theresa walked in dusting off her overalls.

"Hey, you made it," she called cheerfully.

"Billy just dropped me off," I said, "Hope you don't mind if I sit. My ankle is hurting a little."

"Yeah, I heard all about it," she said. She was accompanied by a slender woman with brown hair. Standing next to Ima Theresa, with her great mane of grey tasseled hair, the other woman's brown hair stood out in contrast. The two of them reminded me of salt and pepper shakers.

"Bishop," said Ima Theresa, "I would like for you to meet my partner, Beth Ionesco. Beth, this is bishop Anthony, my boss."

I started to try to stand, but the woman motioned me to remain where I was.

"No, no, please," she said in an accent I couldn't quite place, "don't get up." She came around and shook my hand. "It is very nice to meet you."

"Be careful," said Theresa as she walked into the kitchen, "Elizabeta is Romanian. That's all I'm going to say."

Beth laughed and sat down across from me on the sofa.

"Did you hurt yourself badly?" she asked.

"Sort of," I admitted, "but at least it wasn't broken."

"We heard that you were saved by a good Samaritan," Ima Theresa called from the kitchen. She was putting Martian goat cheese and crackers on a plate and opening a bottle of wine.

"That's true," I called back, "I wouldn't be here if she hadn't come along."

"It was a miracle," said Beth, "They happen all the time on Mars."

"See what I told you?" said Ima Theresa carrying a tray into the living area.

"But it is true," said her partner, "Mars is full of miracles."

"I am beginning to believe that," I said accepting a glass of wine.

"Well, here's to miracles," said Theresa lifting her glass, "After what I am about to tell you, you may be in need of one."

The Bishop of Mars

Chapter Five

"Alima Shariff is coming to Quilong," said Ima Theresa, "She wants to see you before you leave. I think she's pissed off."

It took me a while to absorb what I had just heard. I took a long drink of wine.

"She's coming here," I said, "Why here?"

"We're the nearest town to New Medina," shrugged Ima Theresa, "It's a lot easier for her to come here than go all the way back to Burroughs Base. New Medina is out on the Tempe Terra, the other side of Sharonov."

"Wait a minute, wait a minute," I said, "How do you know her anyway?"

Ima Theresa laughed, "It's a small planet."

I frowned into my drink.

"Look," she went on, "I can't say I really know her. But we've met. The people at New Medina have orchards. They come into town to sell their fruit. So we've talked a couple of times. Very nice woman. And you can't beat those New Medina apples."

"They are really good," Beth agreed.

"But why would she call you?" I asked.

Ima Theresa shrugged again, "I'm a Common Prayer priest. She knew I would get the message to you."

I sat for a moment looking at the two women. I could tell they were not trying to make a joke out of the situation and for that, I was grateful.

"Why is she pissed off?" I asked finally.

"She didn't say. I could just tell by the way she talked. The only other times I have ever spoken to her she seemed very cheerful and friendly. This time she just seemed stressed. She said she would like to see you after church on Sunday before you leave."

I leaned back on the sofa. My ankle throbbed. I sighed.

"It will be ok," said Beth, "She is a very nice person. I am sure you did not mean to offend her."

I looked up.

"So you both heard about me proposing to her?"

They nodded in unison.

"And about *why* I proposed?"

They nodded again.

"You were going to make her honest," said Beth.

"Please, just shoot me," I said.

"Not until after church," said Ima Theresa, "You have work to do tomorrow."

Moses was sitting on two stone tablets. He looked worried.

"What's wrong?" I asked.

"It's these Ten Commandments," he said, "I don't know what to do with them."

"Aren't you going to give them to the Hebrew children?"

"Maybe," he said, "but what if they expect me to live up to them?"

"Would that be so hard?" I asked.

"Have you read them?"

"I see what you mean."

"I'm just the delivery boy," he said, "but I don't think they are going to see it that way."

Ima Theresa and Elizabeta Ionescu run the Mini Martian Day Care Center in Quilong. Five days a week it is full of mini Martians. On Saturdays it serves as a community center for senior citizens. On Sundays it is St. Mary's Church of Common Prayer.

On the Sunday of my visit as the new bishop of Mars the large circular room with the conical roof was packed with people. They sat in chairs in a circle around a table at the center. The table was used by the mini Martians during the week for their art projects; it was stained with a rainbow of finger paint; but with a white covering draped over it, it made a fine altar.

I baptized the babies and confirmed the new church members. I gave a brief sermon since it was such a busy service. As is the custom in the Common Prayer Church, we welcomed everyone to come forward to either take communion or receive a blessing. At the end of the service, the mood was an afterglow of smiles and hugs as people talked about how the smallest of the mini Martians had taken to having water sprinkled on their heads. Holopix pictures were taken of me standing with the proud families and the newly confirmed. I was wearing my bishop's regalia, a cope and mitre, the cape and pointed hat, worn by bishops for centuries.

The bishop and the mini-Martians, tradition and transition, that Sunday at St. Mary's was what church is all about.

Because my coming was something of a community event, people stayed after the service for an open forum. Since my ankle was twinging from having carried my weight for most of the morning, I was given a comfortable place to sit in the inner ring of chairs. The table was moved to the side and used to display the refreshments, apple juice and tea, along with some cookies. The kids were paraded out to play or watch holopix cartoons. I looked at the juice in my cup, wondering if it had started out in New Medina.

Billy Wu introduced me to his community.

"Bishop, we are all wondering where you come down on the Mega

Mars project. There is a great deal of concern about it here in Quilong. We understand the need for tourism on Mars. We've adjusted to that and want to help the Martian economy. But this is different. A lot of people here are worried about how Mega Mars will change our way of life as a non-Vegas planet. And while we are all for the arts, we just aren't sure that the promises match up to the track record. That's why we wanted to host this informal open meeting. We don't mean to put you on the spot. We understand that you have only been on Mars for a short time. But it looks like this proposal is going to come before the Mars Central Authority very soon and we want to hear your views."

I looked around the circle at about 150 expectant faces. They were young and old faces, men and women, people of every color and culture. Quilong is probably the most multi-cultural town on Mars, drawing artistic souls from every corner of the Twin Empires, African Free States or West Hem that can afford to immigrate to Mars. They are an eclectic and eccentric community in Quilong, what an art school would be like if it became a town.

"Well," I began, "I have visited the proposed site for Mega Mars.."

A couple of people snickered softly. I knew most of them had heard about my moronic trip into the desert alone.

"But I guess you have all heard about that…"

A wave of gentle laughter rippled around the circle.

"Anyway, I have given this a lot of thought and I do think I have something I can share."

The room became still.

"As you all probably know, I come from West Hem, probably some of you do too…"

I saw a couple of people nodding their heads.

"I grew up with The Vegas, in Pilgrim's Playground, so I know a lot about how The Vegas operates and I share your concerns. I imagine even those of you who grew up in the Empires can appreciate what I mean."

There was a murmur of agreement from several points on the circle.

"Pilgrim's Playground was the first of the megatainment cities. It was built in a time when West Hem was struggling to find its new life after the Drought. In the beginning, The Vegas took control of this one area and transformed it into a tourist stop for the growing economies of the Empires. The Vegas established order in a time of chaos. They put people to work. So, the promise of new jobs is true."

There were some whispers running like threads around the room, drawing heads together to make comment on what I had just said.

"But the success of Pilgrim's Playground was only the beginning," I continued, "Like dominoes, other cities fell to the expansion of The Vegas. Each time, city by city, The Vegas promised that their casinos would bring salvation to people who were trying to regain what they lost. But in the end, it only brought them under a system that is, well, parasitic."

"What does that mean?" someone across the circle asked.

"It means that The Vegas survives by feeding off of people's needs," I said.

"Like a vampire," a little boy who had stayed with his mother spoke up with a bright expression.

"Yes, like a vampire, that's not a bad comparison," I said. "The Vegas is like a vampire economy. It keeps you alive but you pay a price. It sucks the soul out of whatever it touches."

"Cool," said the little boy. Another quiet ripple of laughter.

A young woman wearing a faded flannel shirt raised her hand. I nodded to her.

"I have a question," she said, "I am from Russia. We have no Vegas in Russia. But if it comes to Mars our government will control it. Won't that be different from what you do in West Hem?"

"Yes," I admitted, "It could be. I know that the Mars Central Authority has said that they will have restrictions on Mega Mars."

"So do you doubt the government?" she asked.

I felt a change in the atmosphere at that moment. An old drug dealer friend of mine had once said, there are two types of people in the world, those who grew up with too little government and those who grew up with too much. In West Hem we have too little. The Vegas lets you do anything you want as long as the right people are getting their cut. In the Empires the story is just the reverse. You are expected to follow the rules. If you do, you are fine. If you don't, you are gone. Questioning the government is a good way to be gone.

"No, of course not," I said firmly, "I am sure the Mars Central Authority has every intention of regulating Mega Mars." I was equally sure that the top bureaucrats were in line for some major bribes too, but I did not say a word about it. One of the unspoken realities of life on Earth is that the virtuous Empires suffer The Vegas to continue because so many of their officials are on the take.

"My worry is that despite the best efforts of our government, The Vegas will find ways to grow their business, even if they have to do it illegally. They will find a way of subverting the regulations. They will promise one thing, but do another."

Many people nodded when I said this. One man from the back raised his hand and then gave voice to the basic question before us.

"So what do we do?"

I took a deep breath. I looked out at the faces around me. Some of those faces I guessed were like me, immigrants from West Hem who knew that challenging The Vegas was a one way trip to the bottom of a cement mixer. Others were immigrants from the Empires, who knew that questioning the government was a quick way to disappear. Suddenly I felt like a guy in the circus. I was about to step out on a tightrope between The Vegas and the Empires. The room was hushed. The safe bet would be to suggest we pass a resolution at our diocesan convention. That could make us feel better, but probably accomplish nothing at all. The dangerous bet would be to take the kind of direct action Ima Maria wanted. That would probably get us locked up as subversives.

Via Media.

Those two words popped into my mind. *The Middle Way.* In the Church of Common Prayer, that's what we claim to be: the church that seeks a balance between extremes, a center path that people from different cultures can walk together. A tightrope over conflict and fear. If there was a via media between The Vegas and the Empires it had to be somewhere between doing nothing and doing too much. Call it divine intervention. Call it inspiration. Call it talking without thinking. I suddenly thought I had an answer.

"I think we ought to circulate a petition," I said. "I think we ought to let the people of Mars speak for themselves."

For just a second my words seemed to drift in the dusty light beneath the high conical roof of Saint Mary's.

"A petition," someone said. It was Billy Wu.

"Yes, a petition," I said again, "Sort of a referendum. We put the question out there and see what the people of Mars think."

"That could work," said Billy slowly, looking around the room. Some people were starting to nod their heads; others were leaning over to whisper to one another.

"It would only be our way of letting the government know how we feel?" asked the Russian woman in the flannel shirt.

"Exactly," I said, "It would be respectful, but clear." The room became a hive of conversation.

"I like it," said Billy Wu, "Let's do it!"

"Well, you may want to give it some…"

I never got to finish my last sentence. The applause was both spontaneous and sincere. Several people were standing. It was as if I had thrown a candle into a pile of paint rags. The artists at Quilong were aflame with the idea of a petition. My idea was the spark they needed to turn their own worries into action. I had come to the town without really understanding how deeply felt the anxiety over the Mega Mars project was, but in the sound of clapping hands filling the Mini Martian Day Care Center, I had found my answer, and apparently, theirs as well.

The meeting went on for almost an hour after I finished speaking. It had a life of its own. Billy Wu took over the organizing work. A steering committee for the petition drive was formed. A ComCom tree for calls to other people in other cities was outlined with different people taking on the task of making those calls. A time table for collecting the signatures was established. I had very little left to do except for one thing: by unanimous acclamation I was to be the author of the petition.

I stood in the corner by the refreshments, now only a sugar graveyard of empty donut boxes and empty cups, saying good-bye to people as they filed out. They shook my hand. They patted my back. They told me I was the voice they had been waiting to hear. Finally, a public figure with the courage to stand up to The Vegas!

When the dust settled, literally because a very fine haze of it floated through the beams of afternoon light coming through skylights at the top of the cone roof, I was alone with Billy, Ima Theresa and Beth.

"You were wonderful," said Beth patting my arm. Ima Theresa stood beside her looking at me quietly.

"Not really," I said, "It was just an idea."

"Oh no," she said, "It was an inspiration. I know everyone will sign your petition."

"Well, it's not really *my* petition…"

"You see," she said smiling, "I told you miracles happen on Mars. Now you go on home with Theresa. I will stay and help Billy clean up."

"Yeah," he said, "You go ahead. Great job, bishop. Just ComCom me the petition when it is ready."

Ima Theresa and I walked out into the afternoon light. I was suddenly glad to be outside. The air felt cool. I would have been happy to walk back to her place but my ankle was throbbing so we drove the short distance to her house. I knew my day was not yet complete. I still had my meeting with Alima Shariff.

Ima Theresa was unusually quiet on the ride. When we got into her house I sat on the sofa and propped my ankle up on a cushion. She brought us each a glass of tea.

"So, what are you thinking?" I asked her.

Her green eyes looked at me from beneath the tangle of grey curls. Her voice seemed deliberate and careful, as if she were measuring out each word with a spoon.

"I'm thinking you just got up on a tiger," she said quietly.

"You don't like the petition idea?"

She took a sip of her tea.

"No, I think that's ok," she said, "It's not as lame as a resolution and it's less of a suicide charge than the one Maria wants to lead." She paused.

"But?" I said.

"But it is still dangerous," she said, "For you."

"You really think so?"

"I know so."

I leaned back and looked at her. Her deep set eyes never wavered.

"This isn't West Hem," I said.

She shrugged, "Different planet, same rules. The bureaucrats are going to be pissed that the petition may blow their cover. They have their hands under the table and they won't like you exposing that. The Vegas, well, The Vegas will be furious that anybody stood up to them. This deal could cost them millions, even billions of Imperial currency. They will want to stop it in its tracks. They will want to stop you."

"But the petition is not just my voice…"

"Doesn't matter. It's your idea. Your name will be all over it. You might as well paint a target on your forehead."

We sat in silence for a moment.

"You really think they would try something here on Mars?" I asked, "I mean something like they do back home?"

Ima Theresa sighed. She slowly leaned toward me, never shifting her gaze from me.

"Do you know what I used to be before I became a priest?"

I shook my head.

"They didn't give you any of the details on us before you came?"

"No," I said, "Just basic stuff. Where you were from. When you went to the Farm. How long you have been here."

"I see," she said in a flat voice, "Well, let me tell you in a word. I was a whore."

I could feel the cold of the glass in my hand. The dome was perfectly silent.

"When I was ten years old I was sold to The Vegas. That was down on the Florida islands, in Everglades. You know the place?"

I nodded. Everglades is where Clare is from. It is a southern version of Pilgrim's Playground, a chain of islands people called the No-Tell Keys because what happens there is kept quiet.

"One day I was playing out in front of this shack of a house I lived in with a dozen brothers and sisters," she said, "The next day I was in the back of a limo being driven to a place you don't even want to know about. I was turned. I was used. I was owned by one the biggest of the big shots who run Everglades. For ten years I was pimped out. Ten years of being nothing but a garbage can. One day, when I was twenty, I ran away. I was older. I was smarter. I had a little money and I thought I could run and hide. I made it all the way to the Dry Lands. I went even farther in than the Farm. All the way to the backend of nowhere. But guess what?"

"They found you," I said flatly.

Theresa never stopped looking at me with her frosted green eyes.

She seemed to take a moment to breathe before she went on.

"I still have the scars. One of the things I love most about Elizabeta is that she says she doesn't mind." She tapped one finger against the table top. "The point is, if you are on The Vegas shit list, there is no where you can run."

I was about to say something. Something about how I understood. Something about how I was sorry for what she had been through. Something about how grateful I was that she had found her way to escape and come into my life on Mars…the whore and the Zappie… but the buzzer on her door let us know that Alima Shariff had arrived. I watched her get up and move across the room. Her grey hair trailing her like the ends of a tattered flag.

Alima Shariff was not alone. I have seen holopix of the men who operate the trade routes around Med Marsh. The man standing beside her looked like one of them. Tall, stern, weathered, dignified. He looked like what a hawk would be if it was turned into a bodyguard. Next to him, Alima Shariff seemed small and she seemed older than I remembered, probably in her forties. That meant that she was still a very young woman. Since the average life expectancy is one hundred twenty, and if she took her boosters which even Naturals like she and I did, then she would be on the very early side of middle age. Her face had none of the lines or creases as the man, but it was just as stern. She wore a headscarf, the hajib, that made her eyes appear even larger, like pools of black water.

"A'Salaam Aleykamm," she said.

I got to my feet and returned her greeting.

"Wa' Aleykam a Salaam."

They both paused. I hoped that my use of the ancient greeting, the exchange of peace, had been polite.

"Won't you sit down?" I asked.

They quietly took their seats. Ima Theresa appeared from the kitchen with two more glasses of tea which she placed before them, then with an excuse of needing to help with the clean-up at the church, she left us alone to talk.

"I am Alima Shariff," she began, "This is my uncle, Kamil."

"I am honored to meet you both," I said, "My name is Tony."

"Yes," she said simply, "I know. You are the bishop of Mars."

"Yes," I said in return, "I am. And I am so glad to have this chance to thank you for what you did for me."

"It is not necessary," she said, "I see that you have recovered."

"I am much better," I replied, "But sincerely, I want to thank you because without you I am not sure I would have survived. You saved my life."

"God saved you," she said, "I was only the instrument of that grace."

I wasn't sure what to say after that. She and her uncle sat upright on the sofa beside one another like two hawks perched on the rim of the desert. Watchful. Waiting. That hawk image was starting to get to me. I felt like a rabbit ten seconds before he got a nasty surprise.

"I have come to ask you a favor in return," she said at last, "I want you to stop telling the story of your rescue as if it were a joke about me."

"I'm sorry," I stammered, "I am not sure I know what you mean."

"I think that you do," she said. Her voice was not raised, but it hardened as she spoke, "Even at New Medina we have heard what people are saying. It is not funny to us. It is hurtful. To me. Personally."

"Oh wait," I blurted out, "I do understand. I have been told what I said to you, when we were in the ambulance, on the way into the hospital. I just meant that I wasn't telling any jokes about it."

"It is not a joke," said her uncle. His voice sounded like a rumble of thunder along the horizon of our conversation.

"I know," I said quickly, "Honestly. It's just that I have these dreams and sometimes I get confused. I must have been on drugs…"

"Pain killers," she said.

"…Yes, and only, this time I was awake, so I said something really stupid. I thought you were someone else. I mean, another woman. It's hard to explain. It's really just a jumble that got stuck in my head. But please believe me, I have not been trying to make a joke out of it."

"I can understand if you were delirious," said Alima, "but I cannot understand why you keep telling the story as if calling me a prostitute was funny."

"But that's what I am trying to say," I stammered, "I haven't been telling it. In fact, it has embarrassed me too. I hate the damn story."

A long moment passed between us. Outside someone went by playing loud music from Mars Radio in their ATV.

Then I had the bright idea to ask, "Weren't there other people in the ambulance when you were driving me into the city?"

"There were. Two rescue techs from the emergency services," she said in a deliberate voice.

"There you go," I said, "I guess on Mars that's all it takes. They must have heard me, and, well, the ball just got rolling."

"What does that mean?"

"I mean, the story, the joke, that whole Mary Magdalene-prostitute thing. It got started."

"It is no joke," repeated her uncle, "It is an insult."

I looked back at Alima and her uncle. I felt flustered. And frustrated. One of the hardest knots to untie is the one that tangles the threads of culture. The myth of Mary Magdalene as a reformed prostitute is a Christian myth. These were Muslims for whom prostitution is synonymous with degradation. Whatever I had babbled in my Zap-style dream about wanting to make an honest woman of her would cause Christians to snicker and Muslims to cringe. Like most knots, the more you picked at it the harder it got to unravel.

"Listen," I said, "This is very hard to explain. We have a story about a woman, Mary Magdalene, in our religious tradition. It is a myth. It isn't true. But it keeps floating around in people's imagination. Apparently, in mine too. Anyway, in my confusion that night I just said some things that were silly…unintentional…but easy to misunderstand. They seem funny to us, but hurtful to you. I really am sorry. Please believe me, I am not trying to make a joke out of any of this. I wish it would go away as badly as you do."

I ended on a breathless note and looked at them with my hopeful rabbit eyes. I am sorry. Please don't eat me.

Alima Shariff regarded me with a grave expression. She took a deep breath.

"Please do all that you can to stop this kind of talk," she said quietly, "I am no prude. I get what happened. But try to see it from my point of view. I am a school teacher. I don't need people laughing behind my back."

"I do understand that."

"And the fact that it is a Christian joke at a Muslim's expense…" she let those words hang in the air between us for a moment, "Mars is too small to let that kind of thing start happening."

"You are absolutely right," I said, "I have respect for your community and would never do anything to cause you trouble. Most of all, I would never mean to insult you. For that, I am deeply sorry. You saved my life. I hope you believe me."

Alima Shariff looked at me through the dark pools of her eyes. I wondered how deep those wells of her soul were. She suddenly seemed so much older than me. Wiser. More mature. All of my insecurities, my sense of still being the street kind called Lucky came rushing back. It made the white choker around my neck tighten. I was not ignorant of the fact that it was a symbol for a past that had not been a sign of the peace we had exchanged when we met. Was her coolness toward me because of our personal history or our cultural history? Or both?

"I believe you," she said. Then slowly she stood up. "We must go now. It is a long journey back to New Medina. I give thanks to God that you are better." She extended her hand.

I stood up and took her hand in mine. If I had had an image of Alima as a hawk, her grip changed my mind. Unlike Digby, these were not bird bones, but the strong grip of a strong woman. We exchanged another salaam. I saw them to the door. They walked out of the dome to climb into a truck, one very much like Billy Wu drove. Just before they departed in a small swirl of dust I saw Alima Shariff look back at me. Her eyes met mine. I started to wave, but they drove off before I could raise my arm. I watched their truck disappear between the Munchkin houses of Quilong. Another beautiful sunset was coming. Another dazzling light show on the Martian cliffs. But I wasn't interested. All I cared about was that she had looked back.

The Bishop of Mars

Chapter Six

"You lied to me."

Abba Ambrose was standing with me in the alley behind the noodle shop. I had called to tell him about the petition when I returned to Burroughs Base. Mr. Chan had given me a chance to talk to him during my break.

"This is outrageous," he said, pointing to the holopix of the petition that glimmered on the ComCom he held in his hand. "You have no right to do this. No right at all."

"I did not lie to you, Abba," I said. "I promised to think it over and I did. In the end I came to the conclusion that the right thing to do would be to let the people of Mars speak for themselves about the Mega Mars project. The petition makes no mention of the church."

"But everyone will know that you are behind it," his long fingers folded up like a dying flower as he hit the off switch on the ComCom pad, "You have given the impression that the church supports this before we have even had our first convention."

"The diocese can still vote on a resolution to support this action or not," I said.

"But don't you see," he cried, "you have already spoken for the diocese even before that vote is taken. You should have waited. You should not have spoken until then. You have exceeded your authority."

Down the alley someone got into a delivery van from the pottery factory, started it up and drove away.

"Now look, Abba Ambrose," I said as evenly as I could manage, "I said that as the bishop of Mars I would abide by the decision of the convention, and I will. If the vote is against our taking a stand on the Mega Mars project I will accept that as the bishop and issue no public statement to contradict it. But as a private citizen I will choose to sign this document if I want to."

"You should have waited for the convention to act," he repeated. His lips were compressed into a tight line.

"There was no time to do that," I said flatly.

Abba Ambrose stood to his full height, like a cobra rising up to strike.

"Do you intend to present this...petition...to the Mars Central Authority yourself?" he asked.

"I intend to be part of a delegation to do so, yes," I answered, "but not as the bishop. I will not wear my shell choker. I will do so only as a private citizen."

"As though that will make a difference," he said. He turned his back to me and walked a few paces away. A gust of wind blew down the alley. The steam from the vent on the noodle shop scented the air. When he spoke again, he did so over his shoulder, "You have exceeded your authority," he said slowly, "You have not only betrayed my trust, but the trust of the diocese."

"If I was trying to betray you I wouldn't have called you to show you the petition," I said, "We just have an honest difference of opinion on this."

Abba Ambrose turned to look at me. In the shadows of the alleyway he looked like a shadow, a shadow come to life. His eyes were narrowed. His face long and pale with anger.

"I intend to make an official protest to the Archbishop," he said coldly, "I shall ask that you be suspended from exercising your duties until a full investigation can be conducted."

I took a breath. I started to say something, but I realized whatever

I said would be translated by his anger into excuses or threats. There was no way to gloss over the divide between us. The petition was a bad review to the opening night of his dreams.

"Then this looks like a case where each one of us must exercise our rights according to our consciences," I said. "You need to do what you need to do, and so do I."

Abba Ambrose took a step toward me. His voice sounded like the steam pipe that came out of the back of Mr. Chan's noodle shop.

"There is widespread dissatisfaction in the church on Earth," he hissed, "There is talk of secession by many parishes and not a few dioceses. I hope your actions here on Mars do not bring that crisis to our planet as well."

The alleyway suddenly seemed hushed. The clatter and clang of the factory and noodle shop suspended in the dusty air.

"It seems to me that that crisis was already here when I arrived," I answered.

We stood like gunfighters facing one another.

"Good day, bishop," Abba Ambrose said.

"Good day," I replied.

He walked down the alley carrying his shadows with him.

I was covered in dirt and breathing hard. Digby, Dr. Wu and I had been hauling boxes of plants up my spiral staircase to the garden. Digby had introduced me to Dr. Wu only the day before. They had appeared at my door when I got home from work, enthusiastic with a plan to transform my roof top desert into an oasis. On my day off we had driven out to the Green Mars Nursery and loaded a trailer with an assortment of berries, vegetables, flowers and even a couple of small citrus trees. I had been anxious about the cost, but Dr. Wu had insisted that it was all taken care of, a welcoming present to me as the new bishop of Mars. Digby pulled the trailer home with his old ATV and we spent a busy morning carrying the trays and baskets up to my roof. My ankle was much improved, but still tender. When the last box had been placed on a shelf, we sat down to take a break.

"I cannot thank you enough for your help," I said as Dr. Wu sat on a crate mopping his brow with a handkerchief. He was Dr. Wu Zhaohui, the foremost terraformer on Mars, friend of Digby, uncle of Billy, and my neighbor. "I have always admired your garden. I noticed it the first day I arrived."

Dr. Wu turned his head to look at the dome of his neighboring garden. He was as compact as Digby. Although I guessed he was some years older, his features were smooth, untouched by the crow's feet and laugh lines that gave Digby his owl-like expression. His hair was a white waterfall of untamed strands that hung far down his small back. A few more wisps of white fell from his chin in the hint of a beard. There was a serenity to Dr. Wu, both in his face and his voice. He was the icon of a Chinese sage. When he spoke, it was like water being turned into words.

"You must come to visit me one day soon," he said, "I am exorbitantly proud of my plants. I would be pleased to introduce you to them."

I looked at the pile of plant trays and bags of loam that cluttered the shelves around us.

"I doubt I will be able to create such a beautiful garden as yours," I said, "I am afraid I don't have much of a green thumb. I grew up in a city where the only plants I saw were weeds."

He laughed softly, "There is no great secret to helping things grow," he said, "It only requires the Tao of listening."

"Same as prospecting," said Digby without turning around from where he was stacking plant boxes.

I dusted my hands off on my overalls.

"I have heard of talking to your plants," I said, "but never listening to them."

Dr. Wu laughed again.

"Oh, but that is essential," he said, "If you listen, they will tell you where they want to be."

"Just like the planet will tell you where the minerals are," said Digby.

Dr. Wu nodded, "Precisely. The Tao of listening is the portal to the ten thousand things." The two older men shared a look that can only be exchanged between friends of long standing. It was a shorthand learned from years of conversation.

"Well, I will do my best," I said. Digby went down the stairs to make some sandwiches while Dr. Wu and I began un-potting the plants. I followed his lead. Slowly the garden began to take shape. I was in awe as I watched his small hands expertly transfer the plants from their box containers into Martian pots, another welcome-to-the-neighborhood gift from the factory next door. These were the same hands that were responsible for reshaping Mars into a new world. As I sprayed water onto rows of green beans I asked him about his work, but he just laughed. I came to understand that laughter was his natural reaction to almost every situation short of illness or death.

"It is not so different from what you do," he said, "I transform land and water. You transform minds and hearts. I think you have the harder job."

"Sometimes it feels that way."

Dr. Wu was placing a small orange tree into a large pot. I helped him set it into the soil.

"My nephew tells me that you are doing great work," he said as we filled in the dirt around the tree. "He tells me that your petition is reaching every town on Mars and causing quite a stir."

"I guess it is," I said truthfully, "but it is not really my petition. The credit really goes to people like Billy. They are the ones who are sending it out across Mars on the ComCom."

"But you are the author, are you not?" he stood up to his small height, stretching out his back after we had gotten the tree in place.

"Yes, I wrote it."

"And it was your vision that brought it into being?"

"Yes, I suppose so."

"Then," he smiled, "You are the critical agent making the change happen. The catalyst. Without you, none of this would have been possible, even if the natural forces have taken over and are now doing the work for you."

I stopped and wiped my forehead.

"Dr. Wu, let me ask you something. Once a process like that has begun, is it true there is no stopping it?"

He sat down on a crate and looked up at me. I noticed a small leaf had decided to decorate his white hair with a tiny splash of green.

"In my work, yes, it is true. In your work, not necessarily. That is why I think what you do is more difficult. And more dangerous."

I sat down.

"What do you mean?"

He rubbed the dirt off his hands and looked across at me. Downstairs I could hear Digby clattering around with the dishes.

"Once I have put natural forces in motion, they cannot really be stopped," he said, "The ice caps melt, the oceans fill, the rain falls. These are natural cycles that are self-perpetuating. With human cycles, it is not so certain. They can always be stopped. Wars happen. Revolutions break out. Leaders die before their time. What people create, other people can destroy." He looked out of my garden dome at the pink light of the Martian day. "What I do is called terraforming. What you do is called history. There is a big difference."

"I have worried that those who want to stop the petition will try to hurt people who are involved in it," I said honestly, "I hope you will tell your nephew to be careful. He seems like such a nice guy."

Dr. Wu laughed softly, "Yes, he is a good guy, as you say. I will tell him to be cautious, but Billy is a grown man who knows his own mind. He believes in what you are doing as do so many others who are signing your petition. No, I don't think they are the ones for whom you should be worried. I think you should be mindful for yourself, my friend, because, as I say, you are the catalyst."

I looked down at the floor for a moment. I have never found it easy to imagine that anyone would want to follow me, especially since I had such trouble managing my own life, but I could see the truth in what he was saying.

"Cut off the head and the body dies," I said. Dr. Wu shrugged.

"Stop the catalyst and the process grinds to a halt," he answered, "That is always the hope and practice of those who want to bend history in their direction. But you know that already from your own religion."

It took me a second, but I made the connection.

"I'm no Jesus," I said.

"And I am no god," said Dr. Wu, "but we both are still responsible for the forces we have set in motion."

I was about to ask him his advice, but Digby's head suddenly popped up above the stairwell.

"You've got company," he said, "There is someone here to see you."

"Who is it?" I asked.

"One of the Russians," was all Digby said and he disappeared down the spiral stairs.

"I will be right there," I called after him. Then turning to Dr. Wu, "Thank you again, Dr. Wu. I am very grateful for your help, and, for your wisdom."

He only laughed and went back to repotting the zinnias.

"His Beatitude, Metropolitan Seraphim, of the Eparchy of Mars, would be honored if you could be his guest for tea," said the Russian priest looking over my shoulder at the painting of Rasputin. He had come to deliver the invitation to me in person, but clearly Mrs. Quigly's art work had captured his attention.

"I would be honored, as well," I said in my best Russian, "What time would this be?"

The priest took his eyes from Rasputin's hypnotic gaze and looked back at me. He was dressed in the long black robe of his office. His chest-length beard was color coordinated with the robe.

"Would four o'clock be convenient?" he asked, a smile softening his austere appearance.

"That will be very convenient," I replied, "Thank you for inviting me."

"I will let the Metropolitan know," said the priest," I am sure he will be delighted."

I showed him to the door, thanked him again, and then let him out. As he walked down the path to the gate I wondered if he would tell Metropolitan Seraphim about Rasputin.

I went into the kitchen. Dr. Wu and Digby were sitting at the table eating sandwiches and drinking fruit juice. I joined them for a quick bite.

"Did you hear all that?" I asked.

They both nodded, cheeks full of food like two hamsters having lunch.

"I guess I better get cleaned up," I said.

"The process is in motion," said Dr. Wu taking a drink of juice, "History is creating itself."

I washed up at the sink. The newer Martian homes have the luxury of private showers, but older places like mine still make do with a single faucet, a reminder of when water on Mars was strictly rationed. I did not have time to go to the public bath house, but I could make myself as presentable as possible with the kind of bath we used to take on the Farm before dinner, just enough to get the grime off and the sweat away.

I was thinking how fast my petition was making waves on Mars. It had been making the rounds for less than a month. If it had gotten me an invitation to see the Metropolitan, who else was starting to notice? Metropolitan Seraphim was one of the most prominent people on Mars. Next to the Co-Governors of the Mars Central Authority, he was probably the most powerful political figure as well. His cathedral, the Cathedral of the Theotokos of Mars, stood just off the Nevsky Prospekt. It looked like a slightly smaller version of St. Basil's in Moscow, a gingerbread of traditional architecture topped by the multi-colored onion cupolas that were so unique to Russian church design. The cathedral was a sign and symbol of the far-reaching influence of the Russian Church.

Why would the Metropolitan of Mars want to invite me to tea? And why now?

The answer was obvious. It was the petition. Compared to Metropolitan Seraphim I was a small fry cleric with a tiny diocese of people I was sure he considered to be misguided Christians at best or heretics at worst. There would be no reason for him to welcome me beneath the onion domes if it wasn't to talk about something he felt was important. And the petition to stop The Vegas was the only thing that could be that important.

"But what does he think about it?" I said out loud.

"What does who think about what?" Digby asked from his perch at the table.

"Nothing. Never mind," I said, going to my room.

As I dressed, I imagined how I would respond if he said that he objected to the petition. What if he told me to call it off? I rehearsed my lines. I thought of how I would stand or sit to seem dignified. I tried to consider some carefully chosen words that would seem persuasive. In the end, I gave up. I realized that I was doing what I always did when I had to encounter authority figures: get anxious, get quiet, feel insecure.

The Russian Church is *the* Church. Big. Powerful. Influential. It is a force of conservatism in religion, just as my church is a force, well, not really a force, but at least a reminder of progressive change. As is common with such inequalities, people fill in the gaps with the stereotypes that make them feel the most comfortable. I was sure that to the Metropolitan, I would seem like a loose cannon. To me, he would be a marble statue. Therefore, I prepared myself for the encounter by indulging my self-righteousness and my prejudice, the two great weapons of ignorance. I got ready to play my part and expected that he would play his.

"Ok, I'm ready," I said to Digby and Dr. Wu who were still talking in my kitchen when I came out dressed in my best clerical garb. I was wearing black trousers and black shoes, the purple shirt of a Common Prayer bishop, buttoned at the neck, with my white shell choker, a simple wooden cross on a string, and a matching purple skull cap. The formal wear for a bishop in our church. "How do I look?"

"Most impressive," said Dr. Wu, laughing.

"Pompously appropriate," said Digby.

"Can I borrow the ATV?" I asked Digby.

"Only if you stay in town," he said with a wry smile.

"I promise," I said, "Say a prayer for me. I think he wants to talk to me about the petition."

"Probably," said Digby, "You are the man of the hour with that petition flying all around Mars."

"I am not sure he sees it that way," I said.

"He is a fair man," said Digby.

"And honest," said Dr. Wu.

And Russian, I thought. I took the keys from Digby and headed out the door.

I drove across town to the Cathedral. It was not hard to find. It is one of the largest buildings in Burroughs Base. The great arches that framed its doors were decorated with images of the Blessed Virgin, the Theotokos, the Mother of God. I parked in a lot next to the church and walked in. As I stepped into the cool interior I could already catch the aroma of incense so typical of Orthodox places of worship. The spicy sweetness filled the air. I walked into the sanctuary to find the young priest with the black beard waiting for me. He welcomed me and together we walked under an enormous dome across a huge open area before the great gilded iconostasis. The iconostasis is literally a golden wall, decorated with larger than life standing icons of Christ, the Theotokos, and other saints, a wall that separates the main worship area from the altar reserved only for male priests. Russian churches have no seats or pews, worshippers stand during the services, so the feeling is of open space, a cavern of sanctity, of beauty, of transcendence. I doubt any person could have walked through this Russian cathedral and not felt in awe. I certainly felt that way.

We walked through hallways covered with portraits of Russian hierarchs along the walls. It was a gallery of men with long white beards, wearing jewel encrusted golden crosses and the distinctive fez-like hats worn by Orthodox Bishops, Metropolitans and Patriarchs. I was suddenly very self-conscious of my wooden cross and handmade cloth skull cap.

Our feet echoed on polished floors. The walls were in a dark plaster. Around every corner silver icons sparkled behind red votive candles, candles arranged in neat rows before the holy images of Mary and Jesus, candles suspended from the ceiling in ornate golden holders. A serene silence seemed to enclose us as we walked. I shuffled along behind the Russian priest, doing my best to breathe in an atmosphere thin with Martian air but rich with frankincense.

I was shown into an office that surprised me. On the long walk through the Cathedral I had been using my imagination to expect the Metropolitan's office as a throne room, but instead it was a large monastic cell. Plain white plaster. A simple icon of the Theotokos. A couple of comfortable chairs. A small table. A larger table used for a desk. The image of the Patriarch of Moscow watched over us from beside a large window that looked out toward a hidden courtyard. The scale was intimate. The impression subdued. From behind the larger table an older man, probably in his early nineties, rose to greet me.

The Metropolitan shook my hand politely, speaking in Russian. I did my best to return the greeting. He showed me to a seat. The young priest placed tea before us. We exchanged a few brief pleasantries about whether I had any difficulty in finding the Cathedral and how I was adjusting to the gravity.

"How do you find Mars?" asked Metropolitan Seraphim.

"It is very different from Earth, Your Beatitude," I said, balancing the glass of tea in my lap, "I think I like it better." It was not the thin green tea of Mars, but rich Russian tea served in glasses with filigreed metal holders. It was as sweet as the smell of incense that permeated his robes.

The Metropolitan gave me a knowing smile. His white beard draped down from a face that reminded me of a male version of Esther Kaminski, but this was a Natural face, untouched by any enhancement other than age, with eyes as dark as the Russian soil. He sat in folds of black cloth, his robe reaching the floor. The only sign of his office was the portrait of the Theotokos he wore on a long silver chain around his neck. His voice was the higher pitched voice of an older man, speaking in Russian with no hint of a Martian accent.

"It is a place still unspoiled," he said, "where the hand of God remains visible for all to see."

"Yes," and remembering what I had said on the flight to Mars, I added, "Like the Garden of Eden."

The Metropolitan seemed as pleased with that image as Esther Kaminski had been. He was nodding as the Russian priest offered to pour him more tea, but he gently waved his hands over his glass. The younger man resumed his quiet station behind the Metropolitan's chair. A bearded angel attending Moses, I thought.

"Beautiful, but still dangerous," said Metropolitan Seraphim, "I understand you had an unfortunate accident."

Self-consciously I crossed my legs and felt my ankle.

"Yes," I said, "a stupid mistake on my part."

"But you are recovered?" he asked.

"Much recovered," I answered, wondering if I had said that correctly in Russian.

"You were blessed with a Good Samaritan," he said with only a hint of light in his eyes. I wondered if there was anything on Mars that this man did not know.

"Yes, I was, Your Beatitude," I said, "a stranger who appeared in the desert to save me."

"And a Muslim, at that," he smiled.

No, there was nothing he didn't know.

I nodded, "Yes, a Muslim."

"A wonderfully spiritual people, the Muslims," said the Metropolitan, "I hope to visit their community at New Medina one day."

"I am sure they would welcome your visit," I said, but the old man just shrugged beneath his robes.

"Insha'Allah, as they would say," he said, "God willing."

"God willing," I repeated and sipped my tea.

"Now let us speak of your petition," he said suddenly. I almost lost hold of my glass. I imagined my reaction was no surprise to him since his timing of the question was so perfect in catching me off guard.

The Metropolitan unfolded his hands and smiled at me.

"I did not mean to startle you," he said, "I am only curious."

"Of course," I said, recovering, "I will be happy to show it to you."

He waved his hands in small circles.

"No need," he said, "I have read it."

The Bishop of Mars

"Oh," I said, and then ran out of words. I looked at him. The Metropolitan held his glass up and the young priest deftly took it and disappeared quietly from the room. From beyond the door of his office I could hear the faint sounds of a choir chanting in the cathedral. Otherwise the room had become very still.

"Your purpose is to ask the government to deny permission to The Vegas to build on Mars, is that right?" he asked. His eyes were fixed on me from beneath their bushy canopy of eye brows.

"In a ..." I struggled for the Russian word, "nutshell, yes." I said.

The Metropolitan smiled and leaned back.

"In a nutshell," he said, "I like that." He paused and then spoke again, "And how do you think the authorities will respond to your request?"

"I am praying they will accept it," I said simply. The Metropolitan gazed at me for a long moment.

"But if your prayer is not answered," he asked, "what will you do then?"

I hadn't thought of that. I fumbled to put my tea glass down on his desk.

"I don't know," I said honestly, "I haven't really thought about it."

The Metropolitan placed his hand on the portrait of the Theotokos.

"You would not condone any violence, I am sure," he said.

"Oh, absolutely not," I said quickly.

"No social unrest or disorder? These things are not tolerated in the Empire," he said.

"I completely understand," I said, "No, our intentions are only to peacefully petition the Mars Central Authority."

The Metropolitan was silent for a long moment, lost in some private thought.

"Many centuries ago, back in Russia, a large number of people petitioned the government," he said, "They were also led by a priest. It was in 1905 by the old calendar. They marched to the Tsar's palace in Saint Petersburg. Their intentions were peaceful, but the outcome was disastrous. Do you know what I am talking about?"

"I'm sorry," I said, "my knowledge of Russian history is…"once again I hunted for the word…"inadequate."

"That is alright," he said, "it is not a part of history of which we are proud. But the lesson remains. Even the best of intentions may have unexpected consequences."

I took a small breath.

"Do you oppose the idea of our petition?" I asked. "Do you think we should not bring it to the Mars Central Authority?"

The Metropolitan glanced at the picture of the Patriarch of Moscow and then back to me.

"The Eparchy of Mars does not take official positions on matters of politics," he said, "The Church is beyond these things. We regard history from a long view, just as I have described, and seek to guide the faithful to learn the lessons that will lead them to God's peace and justice."

"Then, you don't oppose the petition?"

The Metropolitan rose from his chair and at the same moment the young priest reappeared through the door. I realized my audience with Metropolitan Seraphim was at an end.

"Mars is a beautiful creation of the hand of God," he said coming around the desk to bid me farewell, "The Holy Church would never oppose anything that sought to keep it that way." He extended his hand to me. Not being of the Orthodox faith I did not bend to kiss his hand, but I did incline my head as a polite gesture to his office. He laid that hand on my shoulder and spoke in his fine, high voice, "Go with God."

I allowed myself to be shown to the door by the priest. I paused at the door and turned to speak before I left.

"Your Beatitude," I said, "what happened to the priest that led that ancient protest in Russia?"

The Metropolitan turned back to me, resting his hand once again on the portrait of God's Mother that was suspended on the chain around his neck.

"He was swallowed up in a revolution he never intended to create," Seraphim said quietly, "along with all those who followed him."

"I pray that will never happen here," I said.

"Insha'Allah," said the Metropolitan, "God willing."

As I drove away from the Cathedral of the Theotokos, the late afternoon sun was throwing carpets of shadow across the roadway. The multi-colored onion domes caught the dying light as if it might never come again.

I was half paying attention to my driving because my mind kept going over what Metropolitan Seraphim had said to me. It was not at all what I had expected.

I had imagined a dour and uncompromising ideologue sitting on a throne admonishing me to abandon my part in the petition drive to stop The Vegas. My prejudices against the Orthodox Church had painted a caricature of the Russian hierarchy. And while Metropolitan Seraphim had certainly looked the part, he was no ecclesiastical demagogue. Instead, he seemed like a wise but cautious grandfather…if the grandfather was also a master politician.

Was I like the priest of his history? Was I leading a suicide protest into chaos? Was the petition a mistake?

I was letting these questions spin around the rinse cycle of my brain and driving on autopilot when I looked in my rear view mirror and saw the flashing blue lights of a truck following me. Only one kind of vehicle on Mars flashes blue lights, the Mars Authority Constabulary. These were MACs, Martian cops. I must have been asleep at the wheel and committed some traffic violation. I pulled over.

I was fumbling in my pants pocket to find my ID badge when a MAC officer stepped up next to Digby's ATV. His face was covered by a dark visor.

"I'm sorry, officer," I started to say.

"Please step out of the car," he said in Russian, thick with a Martian accent.

"What did I…"

"Step out of the car," he repeated. By the way he filled out his black overalls I knew he was a good head taller than me and twice as wide, but just in case he needed back up, his equally large partner appeared on the other side of the ATV. I climbed out and started to hand them my ID.

The officer nearest me took my elbow in a vice grip and began pulling me toward their truck.

"Come with us," he said. His partner fell in along on the other side, taking me by my other arm.

"Well, ok, but where are we going?" I stammered, feeling as if my shoes were just scraping the top of the ground. The street around us was almost empty of traffic. I looked around quickly but saw no one else but a lonely delivery van turning a far corner.

"Get into the truck, "said the MAC.

"But what have I…"

"Into the truck," he said and shoved me through a door into the back seat. He slammed the door. He and his partner got into the front seat and without a word they drove away, leaving my ATV sitting by the side of the road.

"Look you guys," I said leaning forward, "if I have broken any laws…"

But I never finished my sentence. The MAC on the passenger's side turned around silently, holding a gun directly into my face. He never spoke. He didn't have to. I had seen enough of guns in Pilgrim's Playground to know that silence is the best response when the other end of the argument is a bullet through your brain. I sat back and let them drive me to an industrial area in the city. At first, I tried to remember landmarks, but I was too scared to pay attention. Having grown up in Pilgrim's Playground I knew that it didn't really matter if these men were cops or not. Either way, I was in trouble.

They pulled up to a large metal door that swung open when they sounded their horn. The truck slid into the building, the door closed, and the driver cut his engine.

"Get out," he said. I didn't argue. I stepped out of the back of the truck into the gloom of a warehouse. I could feel my knees shaking. I wanted to pee.

The two MACs walked toward me. I held up my hands in front of me.

"Look I don't want any trouble," I started to say.

"Too late," said one of the MACs.

The other one hit me in the stomach.

A Russian priest was crying in the snow. Around him were the bodies of scores of men, women and children. They had been shot. Their blood speckled the snow with splashes of red.

I knelt down beside him.

"What happened here?" I asked.

He looked up at me. His face was haggard and lean, the long beard that hung from it drooped like a flag fallen in surrender. His eyes were so red from crying they looked like blood on snow.

"The Tsar wasn't even at home," he said weakly, "We came to bring him our petition and he wasn't even at home."

I looked out over the field of bodies. They lay before the gates of the Winter Palace in Saint Petersburg.

"Were you their leader?" I asked.

"No," he said looking down, "I was their catalyst."

Chapter Seven

Archbishop Clare's face looked worried. Even in the flickering holo-light of a long distance transmission I could see her yellow eyes wrinkle like flowers closing against a storm.

"Are you alright?" she asked.

I tried to squeeze my swollen face into the semblance of a smile.

"I'm fine," I said, "I feel better than I look."

She stared back at me with a look that said she wasn't convinced.

"Maybe this isn't a good time to talk," she said.

"No, it's fine," I replied, "And considering what a long distance call costs we had better not waste it talking about my ugly mug."

"Forget the cost," she said with a frown, "it's you I am worried about. How did this happen?"

"According to the official version? I was driving recklessly. Went off into a ditch. No seat belt. Flipped out and injured myself."

"And the real version?"

"Classic Vegas. They beat my ass."

"Because of the petition?" she asked.

"Had to be," I said.

Ima Clare looked at me intently through the blue haze of the ComCom link. I sat upright in my hospital bed. The same room I had been in before.

"Are you getting good care?" she asked.

"I am becoming a regular," I said.

"It's not funny," she snapped.

"Sorry. Yes, very good care. Actually, much better than I would have gotten at home. These are Imperial doctors here. I look like I lost the fight, but I will be ok."

"Damn it," she said. She looked away from the screen and then turned back. "You could have gotten yourself killed."

"I know," was all I could think to say, "I realize that now, but I had to do something. The petition seemed like the best choice."

"So what is happening with it now?"

I leaned back on my pillows and watched Clare's image float above the arm tray over my bed.

"It's gotten a lot of signatures," I said, "although that may slow down now. I am sure what happened to me will cause some people to think twice before signing."

"Will you still take it to the Mars Central Authority?"

I stared back at her image. The blue light brought back bad memories of the MACs who had pulled me over… if they were MACs.

"Lucky?"

"Yes, sorry. I…I don't know. I've asked the others to hold off. We had planned to present it to the government just before The Vegas lawyers arrived, but I don't want anyone else to get hurt. Anyone who carries it in could be making themselves a target. I don't know. Maybe I will do it on my own."

"Now listen to us very carefully," Ima Clare said, "We do not want you to do that. Is that clear?"

I felt my shoulders tense as I leaned forward toward the ComCom. "Is that an order?"

"If it has to be," she said, "We don't want you getting killed."

"So what should I do? Just tear up the petition and say, never mind? Just let The Vegas march in and build their goddam casino?" I realized I was starting to shout. I sat back and tried to breathe.

Clare remained quiet for a moment. When she spoke her voice had lost its edge.

"Lucky, please," she said, "I know this is not an easy time for you. But doing a one man martyr mission against The Vegas is not going to help. People are aware of the petition without you're having to hand-deliver it. It has made the news up there and it has certainly made it down here."

"What do you mean?" I asked.

Clare pursed her lips together, as if she were reluctant to add more misery to our conversation.

"Well," she said slowly, "you need to know that there has been an official call for me to suspend you."

"I'm not surprised. I was expecting that."

"I will have to treat it seriously," she said.

"I was expecting that too. I understand."

"They do have a case," she said quietly, "You acted unilaterally without the support of your convention. You did not seek my approval as Archbishop. In effect, you went solo. They say you are a loose cannon and that I am responsible for appointing you as a radical priest with a bad track record."

I felt dizzy and it wasn't from pain killers. Her image seemed to swim in a pool of blue water.

"Oh shit," I said, "I am so sorry."

Clare regarded me through the pixel points carrying our faces across space. She chose her next words carefully.

"The political situation back here is delicate," she said, "The conservatives are threatening to leave the church and take as many dioceses with them as they can. They are going to be watching what I decide to see if I give them an excuse."

I didn't wait to reply.

"If you need to suspend me, or dump me, or whatever, go ahead," I said, "I won't contest it and I probably deserve it."

"Slow down," she said sharply, "One step at a time. I am playing for time here. We are not…I am not going to be stampeded into any action until things calm down up there. When is your convention?"

"Next week," I said. I suddenly felt exhausted.

"Take this whole situation to them. Have them pass a resolution of support for you. At least we will have some firm ground to stand on. Do you think you can do that?"

I nodded, "I think most of the diocese is with me. But it will be after The Vegas lawyers are here to talk business with the Mars government. It will be after the fact."

"That can't be helped," she said crisply, "We're in no position to fight this thing if you do anything without some form of official church sanction."

"Alright," I muttered, "I get it. I understand."

"You sure you are ok?" she asked quietly.

"I am," I said.

"I am…we are…sorry, Lucky," she said, "I wish it didn't have to be this way. You did your best."

"Yeah," I said, "Don't worry about me. Just do what you need to do."

"I will let you know what I decide before the convention," she said softly, "Until then, take care of yourself and try to stay out of trouble."

"Sure," I said, "Thank you for the call."

"God bless you, Lucky," said Ima Clare. Her face vanished in the blue shimmer of a light cut off in the cold space between Earth and Mars.

I was sitting in my kitchen trying to decide what to do with all of the baskets of mushrooms I had collected over two stays in the hospital when Digby called to give me some more good news. He was on his way out to some unspecified location.

"You've been fired from your job," he said, "Mr. Chan is sorry, but he can't help it."

"When it rains it pours," I said looking at the portrait of Rasputin on my living room wall. He looked like I felt.

"What does that mean? We don't get much rain on Mars."

"Bad things come in three's," I replied, "but who's counting?"

He signed off with a promise to check in on me when he got back. I looked over at Rasputin again.

"What are you laughing at?" I said out loud and went back into the kitchen.

I went up the spiral staircase to my roof garden. I took a small watering can, filled it, and began tending the plants that Dr. Wu had so carefully arranged for me. The dome was filled with the soft pink glow of a Martian morning. Outside the dome I could see the factory workers stacking pots in a storage area. I glanced over at Dr. Wu's garden. It was alive with green fronds and flowers. I imagined him off on some other call to transform Mars into just such a garden. How long would that take? Centuries? Millennia? I didn't know, but at least he would always be remembered as a catalyst for good. As for me? I sighed. I was having a good dose of the self-pity blues. I slumped onto a crate. I looked at the plants. Tiny beads of water glistened on their leaves.

"Ok," I said, "I'm listening. Tell me what to do."

The ComCom chirped an in-coming call. This seemed like my day for Com calls. I flipped it on. It was Ima Theresa. She seemed uncharacteristically breathless.

"Are you watching the news?" she asked abruptly.

"No, I'm…"

"Well turn it on," she said and clicked off.

I hurried down the stairs and turned on the ComCom in the living room. Mars only has one channel so it wasn't hard to catch the news report. A reporter was standing on a street. Behind her, a block away, there was a cluster of blue lights and the sounds of people shouting. Several figures raced past her. An ambulance drove toward the screen and then disappeared down a side street, its klaxon almost drowning out her voice.

"A scene of chaos," she was saying in a loud voice, "as several of the protesters have been forcibly ejected from the Saint Vladimir City Hall. We can confirm that at least three of the rioters have been injured. MAC officials tell us that two constables have suffered injuries and will be taken to hospital."

"Can you give us any more details about how many protesters were involved?" a male voice asked. I guessed it was the news anchor back in the studio. She pressed her hand against an earpiece and glanced over her shoulder.

"We think about a dozen," she said, "but reports are sketchy. All we can say for certain is that the ringleader appears to be a woman who has a known history of confrontation with the police. She is Maria Standing Bear, apparently a local union organizer and religious leader."

"Is this directly connected to the recent petition drive?"

"That's right," shouted the reporter over the sound of more klaxons in the background, "Maria Standing Bear was the local organizer of the petition drive. But how this brought her and her followers to attack City Hall remains to be seen. We will stay with the story."

The scene suddenly shifted to the familiar face of the local news anchor, a carefully tailored Chinese reporter with the features of a ComCom soap star.

"In related news," he said, "lawyers just arrived from West Hem say they are shocked, but not surprised by this recent turn of events."

Two beautifully manicured female lawyers in severe grey business suits appeared on screen. I was about to listen to their interview when my hand held ComCom chirped again. I muted the sound and took the call. It was Theresa.

"Did you see it?"

"I'm watching it now," I said, "They named Maria. What the hell is going on?"

"After she heard what happened to you," she said, "Maria and a group of her steelworker buddies decided to take the petition down to the city hall at Saint Vlad. That's the word I get from people in the parish. Apparently things got out of hand. The MACs tried to block the entrance. A shoving match started. Some punches were thrown. You can figure out the rest."

"Have they arrested her?"

"You bet," said Ima Theresa, "Disturbing the social order. A felony in both Empires."

"Oh God," I said, "I can't believe this is happening."

"You have to believe it," said Ima Theresa, "because if it is happening to her, it is happening to you."

"What do you mean?"

"I mean get a lawyer," she said, "because according to Imperial law if Maria is charged with crimes against the social order, her superiors will be charged as well. They will hold you responsible for her behavior."

I sat for a moment, just looking at her.

"Bishop?" she said, "Did you hear me?"

"Yes," I said quietly, "I heard. I understand. Thanks for the warning. I need to get off now. If I don't talk to you before, I'll see you at convention."

We hung up. I sank back onto the sofa and let the ComCom video images play on mute. More scenes of the riot. More scenes of MACs or protesters being taken off to hospital. More reporters standing before the crowd. More pictures of The Vegas lawyers looking beautiful and deeply concerned. I watched for most of the afternoon. But I never turned the sound up.

One day, when I was a teenager living on the streets in Pilgrim's Playground, I took the magtrain out into the suburbs. I had never been there before. It was like going to another planet. Perfect lawns in front of perfect houses with perfect people doing perfectly perfect things.

I slouched through open air shopping areas marveling at how clean it all looked. And smelled. This was the land of plenty. It was a place where nothing bad ever happened. Or at least, that is what it seemed like to me. I window shopped along a row of expensive stores, stores that sold things I had only stolen. Eventually, I retreated from all of this oppressive perfection after too many unfriendly looks by the locals. In my black vinyl pants, greasy hair and pink pointed shoes (yes, I wore them) I stood out too much and felt like a leper crashing a garden party. I got back on the magtrain and returned to the litter, smog and noise I called home. That was my first taste of what I came to call the perfect burbs.

New Shanghai was my second.

It is the perfect burbs of Mars. While there are no green lawns or golf courses, there are neatly tailored houses with large enclosed courtyards and three car garages. There are no windmills in the neighborhoods. The local power system is a state-of-the-art wind and solar farm located outside the city so that nothing disrupts the skyline of egg-shaped garden domes. These gardens are tended by an army of landscape technicians who move from house to house along with the cleaning services that keep New Shanghai interiors spotless. The streets are not the winding dusty roads of Burroughs Base, but well laid out tarmac avenues, swept clean by a fleet of sand sweepers that crawl like giant bugs between the freshly painted walls of the houses. Each one has the logo of a little green man pushing a broom, smiling.

New Shanghai had the first true shopping mall I had seen on Mars. It is an arcade of Roman vaults, lined up over four long blocks, covered by a massive dome that not only keeps the interior dust free and temperature controlled, but pipes in alternating Russian and Chinese folk songs. Many of the stores are specialty import shops where affluent citizens can buy the latest Earth fashions. There is even a restaurant that serves the most exotic food on Mars, meat. Martians are vegetarians. The planet does not support livestock. Only the jaded and privileged few flaunt this reality by consuming the status symbol imported from Home World, hamburger.

"It's really gross," said Abba Isidore's wife, Kalisha.

She was driving me to Saint Anselm's church, the Common Prayer parish that was the site for my first church convention as the bishop of Mars. I had missed meeting her at my clergy dinner because she had to work. Kalisha is the principal of the Venerable Bede Academy, the only private school on Mars. Like her husband, she was young, energetic and hopeful. At least, until I showed up.

The ride in had been very subdued. I looked at New Shanghai through the windows of her ATV as Kalisha brought me in from the airport. She had been working hard to ignore my black eye. She never asked me how it had really happened. Given the fact that Ima Maria was in jail, along with several of her parishioners, I had decided to keep my own troubles to myself.

I had called Maria, of course. I may have been the one call she was allowed to receive, I'm not sure, but when we talked she was as fiery as ever. Jail did not seem to have dampened her spirit.

"They started it," she said, "We are being framed."

"That may be, Maria," I told her, "but this felony charge is no joke."

"We haven't been officially charged yet. That may take a few more days."

"But is there any doubt they will charge you as subversives against the social order?"

Ima Maria was quiet. I could hear voices in the background. She was talking from a jail ComCom.

"No," she said finally, "no doubt." We were both quiet for a moment, then she added, "And if they do…when they do…charge me, they will come after you next. That's how it works."

"I know," I said.

"Please believe me," she started to say, "I never meant for any of this..."

But she never got to finish. She was cut off. Her time up. Maybe it was up for us both.

I entered St. Anselm's like a dead man walking. It was, as I had suspected, a perfect church for the suburbs. We walked through an archway into a lovely courtyard of Martian tile, complete with a statue of St. Francis feeding the birds, if there were any birds on Mars, which their aren't. The church itself was spacious, open and inviting. A small fountain of water gurgled away at the entrance to the sanctuary.

"This is where we do baptisms," Kalisha explained, but given my mood, I barely noticed.

For the next several minutes I endured the looks of the men and women I met as Kalisha introduced me. They studied my face as though trying to read a map. I imagined my swollen eye gave me a sinister look. I kept seeing people staring at it as they tried to make small talk. They were doing their best to welcome me, but I felt as if I were walking through the suburbs as a teenager in Pilgrim's Playground again. I stood out. I was wrong for being there.

Because of me, what should have been a family reunion was a funeral. Because of me, Ima Maria was in jail. Because of my petition, the church was being portrayed as a breeding ground for radicals. I had made us pariahs. No one said anything directly, but I could feel the tension. I was their bishop and all I had done for them was make trouble.

Finally Abba Isidore came gazelle-leaping around the chairs set up for the meeting to pump my hand.

"Are you ok?" he asked quietly. His gentle African features radiated concern.

"Yes, I am fine," I replied, realizing that my self-consciousness must be more obvious than a pair of pointed pink shoes.

"Well, come on into my office and rest a little. I bet you are really worn out by the trip."

I wondered if I looked that bad, but let him lead me to a back office where I sank into a soft cushioned sofa that looked out into a secluded part of the courtyard. St. Francis was feeding imaginary birds.

"Just take it easy for a while," Isidore said, "I will come to get you when it is time."

"Do people know what happened to me?" I asked before he left, "Do they know why I look so bad?"

"You don't look all that bad," he said, "You've got a black-eye. Some people think it was a car wreck, but most suspect the truth."

"Are they afraid?"

Abba Isidore paused before he answered.

"Sure, but they still have faith in you as their bishop. They believe in you. So get a little rest and you can talk to them when they all get here."

He smiled as if he were trying to give me a gift, convince me of a hope I still could not receive, and then he stepped out of the room and closed the door.

Saint Francis and I were sitting in a duck blind beside a still lake on an early morning. He was wearing a camouflage vest over his brown robe. He lifted a duck call to his lips. Its eerie baawack-baawack sound echoed over the lake.

"What are we doing..."

"SSShhhhhh," he hissed, motioning me to silence with one hand. In the other he held a shotgun.

Baawack-Baawack.

"What are we doing here?" I whispered close to his ear.

Saint Francis never took his eyes from the sky.

"Got to put some meat on the table," he whispered.

Baawack-Baawack.

I watched as he brought the shotgun up to his shoulder.

"You are a hunter?" I whispered in amazement.

"Disappointed in me?" he asked.

"Well, yeah, a little."

"So now you know how they feel about you."

Then he pulled the trigger. The fiery explosion of the shotgun ripped open the still morning air.

"Sorry, did I wake you?"

I rubbed my eyes. Kalisha was standing in her husband's office, balancing a stack of reed-paper books in her hands. They were the prayer books unique to our church, the source of our name as the people of Common Prayer.

"I dropped one on the coffee table," she said apologetically.

I got to my feet.

"Here, let me help you," I said.

We carried the prayer books out to the parish hall. Convention delegates from all four churches were already in small clusters of conversation. Their voices were subdued. They cast furtive looks around the room. It felt like we were gathered for the reading of a will. Ima Theresa looked at me from across the room. Her delegation of artists from Quilong looked like brightly colored birds who had been through a heavy rain. Dampened. Still. Uncertain.

Abba Ambrose and his entourage were already seated. A jury of Puritans. Stiff and stern, prepared to hear the worst and dispense spiritual justice without flinching. They avoided eye contact with me as I moved around the room trying to speak to as many people as I could. But the weight of small talk felt even heavier than usual for an introvert like me, so I found a corner where I could talk with Kalisha about a few trivial matters that would make me look busy.

"The room feels empty without Ima Maria," she said sadly.

I looked over at the steelworkers who had come on short notice to take the place of those who had been arrested. They all were trying to look brave, I thought, but without Maria they seemed like very big kids sitting in chairs far too small for them.

"It sure isn't the convention I had imagined," I said quietly.

Kalisha placed a hand on my arm.

"I know, but you mustn't blame yourself for what has happened." I looked into her eyes, feeling a warmth in her look that held me for a moment in the chill of the room. "You did the right thing, bishop."

"Maybe," I said, "but look at what it cost Maria. And her people. And the whole church."

"Maria is a grown woman," said Kalisha with a sternness that caught me off guard, "She made a choice and followed her conscience. Now, like you...like all of us...she will have to deal with the consequences."

"Wow, Kalisha, you surprise me. That's a hard ass way to look at it."

Kalisha looked back at me with an expression that matched the strength of her words. It was not a suburban look. Not the perfect expression of a perfect person in a perfect world, but the face of an African woman whose ancestors had survived for centuries because they didn't flinch when things got hard.

"Don't judge a book by its cover, Tony."

"I think I am beginning to learn that," I said, "Thank you for your help, Kalisha, and for your honesty."

"Any time," she said, giving my arm a squeeze.

I was welcoming the steelworkers from Maria's parish when Abba Isidore came across the room. He excused himself for interrupting us and pulled me aside.

"This just came in from Home World," he said, handing me his portable ComCom. "It's for you and it's marked personal."

I looked at the small glowing screen of the hand-held ComCom. It was marked as an official message from the Office of the Archbishop, labeled personal to the Bishop of Mars.

"Thank you," I said.

He turned to go, but stopped and looked back at me.

"I just want you to know, bishop," he said quietly, "That whatever it is, I will support you one hundred percent."

"Thank you, Isidore," I said, "That means a lot to me."

He nodded and walked away. I punched the keys and read the message:

Sorry to send this to you last minute but I have tried every option I could. An official statement announcing your suspension as the Bishop of Mars follows. You can show that to the convention. It is effective immediately. I have no other choice. What you don't know on Mars has leaked out here on Earth. Apparently the Mega Mars deal has been stalled. Someone up there is putting pressure on the Mars Central Authority. Big pressure behind the scenes. The Vegas is furious. They are blaming you. That means they are also blaming us. Blaming me. They are threatening to shut down our parishes with an avalanche of code violations, building inspections, energy use permits, etc. The conservatives are panicked. They say you will be the ruin of the church. Your petition is the only visible target for causing the trouble and you are at the center of that target. I need to buy time to get on top of this before it pulls the house down around my ears. I know you will understand. Clare.

P.S. Don't use any church ComCom link to reply after you get this. And above all, be careful.

I stared at the screen for several minutes. I re-read the message then deleted it. My legs felt like rubber. I rubbed my eyes. My face ached. I felt queasy in my stomach. I wanted to go back to Abba Isidore's office to sit on his sofa so I could think. But Ima Theresa was suddenly standing behind me, her voice pulling me back into the room.

"We're ready, bishop," she was saying.

I turned slowly to see her staring at me. Behind her the last delegates were taking their seats. Abba Ambrose was sitting on the front row. He was staring at the ComCom in my hands as though he could read it by telepathy.

"Whoa," she said, her eyes going wide, "are you ok? No offense, Tony, but you look like you could pass out."

"Do I look that bad?" I mumbled.

"Not if you're a vampire who has never been in the sun, otherwise you are the palest Irishman I've ever seen. Do you need to sit down?"

I waved her off.

"No, no, I'm alright," I said, "I just got some bad news."

Ima Theresa looked down at the ComCom.

"From Archbishop Clare?" she whispered. I nodded.

"This isn't going to be easy," I said, "but it won't take long. This will probably be the shortest convention in church history."

"Oh shit," she said, "she's had to suspend you."

I didn't answer her. I just reached over and squeezed her hand. Then I walked to the podium and rapped on it to call the meeting to order.

"Ok," I said, "let's get started."

The room fell silent.

"Brothers and Sisters…

" I said.

"Could you speak a little louder?" someone from the back row called out.

"Sorry," I said clearing my throat, "Brothers and Sisters, I have an important message to share with you, but before I do, I think we should begin with a prayer."

All the heads in the room bowed like trees bent by a strong wind.

"Let us pray," I said.

I never meant it more.

The Bishop of Mars

CHAPTER EIGHT

When I got home Rasputin was laying on the floor. He stared up at the ceiling through broken glass. The rest of my house was not in much better shape. My clothes had been turned out onto the floor. The furniture was tipped over and broken. Even the kitchen drawers had been emptied into piles of silverware strewn across the Martian tiles.

The worst damage was in the garden. My poor plants looked as if they were victims of a Martian dust devil. The strawberries were bleeding onto the floor, crushed beneath whoever's feet had upended the trays and pots, spilling black loam from the nursery among the twisted remnants of flowers and vegetables.

I called the MACs, of course. They came out to walk through the wreckage and file a report. RANDOM VANDALISM I saw one of them write on a ComCom notepad. When they left I sat alone on the one kitchen chair that wasn't bent and cried.

People might imagine an addict like me would be too hardened by my life to cry. They might think I got the crying beat out of me as a kid. They might think if you are poor you are used to hurting. No more tears left.

Bullshit. The poor cry because they have good reason to cry.

But I wasn't just crying for myself. I was crying for the people whose faces I had seen when I projected Archbishop Clare's official message on a screen in the parish hall.

Effective immediately, Abba Anthony is suspended from his duties as the Bishop of Mars. Until my arrival to conduct a full inquiry the diocese will be under the care of the Standing Committee chaired by Abba Ambrose. Signed, Ima Clare, Archbishop.

The room was absolutely silent after that message. The only sound was Kalisha crying softly in the corner. Ima Theresa had taken charge. She said that the Standing Committee, a combined committee of representatives from each parish and the clergy, would meet soon to make decisions about the future. Given the situation, the diocese would wait for the arrival of the Archbishop. People began to get up to leave as if they were sleepwalking. Only Ambrose had remained seated, an unmoving presence in the midst of the chaos.

I had limped home on the last scheduled flight of Mars Air before the dirigibles were hangared for the duration of sand storm season. I took a taxi home and walked into more pay back. Given what I had done to the diocese over my first few weeks as bishop, I felt I deserved it.

I wiped my eyes and wished Digby would come around the corner to comfort me. But I knew that wouldn't happen. The only scrap of paper not ripped up had been a small note taped to the refrigerator door. It wasn't signed but I knew it was from Digby. "Gone prospecting" was all it said.

I thought about calling someone else, but who? Ima Theresa? Abba Isidore? ...but what would I say? Come hold my hand?

No, they were dealing with the shock waves my actions had set in motion in their own communities. They had enough to cope with, thanks to me. They had to hold the church together. I wasn't going to add to that burden. I would handle this mess on my own.

But how?

Be careful, Clare had said, but how was I supposed to be careful? You can't hide from The Vegas. Not on Earth and not on Mars.

Maybe I should just resign, I thought. Renounce the priesthood. Catch the next transit ship to Home World. Disappear into the slums where I belong. Take a hit of Zap.

That last thought shocked me out of my self-pity. I hadn't had an idea like that in years. I had locked those things away in a basement and swallowed the key. It scared the shit out of me to think they would come back. Especially now.

"May I be of help?"

I looked up to see Dr. Wu standing in the kitchen door, his small face grave with concern.

"Yes, please," was all I could think to say.

He did not speak but only extended his hand to help me up. I picked up my travel bag and followed him out of the wreckage of my house, not knowing where else to go.

"You must leave the city," said Dr. Wu.

We were sitting by candle light in the sanctuary of his roof top garden. The flickering light cast shadows across our faces beneath the hanging leaves.

"It is not safe for you here. There are strange things happening. There is a rumor that the government is being pressured by the banks not to go through with the Mega Mars project."

"Because of the petition?" I asked. "Because of me?"

Dr. Wu pulled his eyebrows together over the smooth surface of his face. His eyes glistened like black pebbles in a clear stream.

"Yes and no. Your petition is the catalyst," he said, "But it has set in motion other forces that are now frustrating The Vegas plan. Forces that are not transparent. Something else is at work."

"What?" I asked, but Dr. Wu only frowned and shook his head.

"I do not know. It is all very mysterious. Very hidden." He placed one small hand on my arm. "But you... you are not hidden. You are the visible symbol of this trouble and The Vegas is looking for someone to blame."

I rubbed my hands over my face as if trying to clear cobwebs off my skin. My right eye still felt tender to the touch.

"So what do I do?" I asked.

"You disappear," he said firmly, "You get out of the city. You hide."

Suddenly, with the irrationality of testosterone, I felt ashamed.

"I'm not running away," I said, "I will stay here and…"

"And do what?" asked Dr. Wu, "Get killed?"

I looked down. The leaves of his garden draped like banners of a beaten army around me.

"You can do nothing more here," he said quietly, "except create a distraction for your friends and a target for your enemies."

He was right. I was no longer the Bishop of Mars. I had no authority. I had no political clout. I didn't even have any religious credibility. Clare would not be coming to Mars until she could put out the fires burning the church down on Earth. Fires I had started. That could take weeks. Maybe months. In the meantime, my visible presence in Burroughs Base only gave The Vegas another opportunity to frighten the public into silence. The real power was moving behind the scenes. Wheels were turning, but I could not control them.

"Ok," I said, "I understand. I'll lay low for a while. I'll go underground."

Dr. Wu placed one of his small hands on my shoulder.

"It is a wise choice," he said, "Live to fight another day."

"But where will I go?" I asked, "If I go to stay with any of my friends, at any of our parishes, I will only be putting them in danger."

Dr. Wu stood up. He looked out through the dome to the alley behind our two houses. I wondered if he thought we were being watched.

"There is an alternative," he said with his back to me, "There are contacts I have that can be trusted for their discretion. It is a risk for them, but they may be willing to take it. They will get you out of the city and put you in touch with others who will hide you. Others that The Vegas will not suspect."

He turned to look at me. Seated on my stool, I was almost as tall as he was standing.

"Thank you," I said looking into his eyes.

"You are welcome," said Dr. Wu smiling gently in the dim light.

"I guess I have made a royal mess out of everything," I said.

"That remains to be seen," said Dr. Wu, "The Tao that is seen is not the true Tao. We must have faith."

"Well," I sighed, standing up and taking a deep breath, "sometimes that's all you've got left to go on."

Dr. Wu bowed ever so slightly.

"And sometimes that is all you need," he said, blowing out the candle.

The next night I was bundled into thermal overalls, the kind Martians use when they travel by night. It had insulated boots and gloves, a pull over hood and a face mask that covers everything but the eyes. With night vision goggles I could walk easily in the dark, but be unrecognizable if seen. Dr. Wu had made me stay indoors during the day while he made what he called "arrangements". At midnight he had given me the outfit I was wearing and his instructions.

"Go to the end of the alley. Cross the street. Go down the next alley for two blocks. Wait for a black truck without markings."

"Thank you," I said, "I don't know how to repay you for helping me."

"If a gift is given freely it needs no repayment," was all he said.

I followed his instructions, darting across the more lighted spaces of the roadway, keeping to the shadows. It was the first hour of a Martian morning. Phobos was just completing its rapid run across the Martian sky. There were no people out at this hour so I felt fairly certain

THE BISHOP OF MARS

that I was not seen.

I stood against a wall, waiting for the black truck. I had my travel bag with me, still packed from my trip to the convention. After my mini-breakdown back at the house, I had regained some of my confidence. At least I was doing something. Dr. Wu was right. If I stayed in the city I would just sit in the ruins of my home brooding about my failures.

I shivered in my padded jumper and thought about the Martian desert. COMING SOON. I could see the sign flashing in my mind. No, I didn't regret trying to stop that. Maybe the petition wasn't able to halt the project completely, but it had thrown sand in the gears of The Vegas. It had stirred up something, or someone, enough to rattle The Vegas and that was not an easy thing to do.

Just then I saw two headlights swing around the intersection by the city park. A black van cruised slowly down the street and glided to a halt only a few meters from my hiding place. I didn't hesitate. I stepped out of the shadows quickly, opened the back door of the van, tossed my bag in and jumped after it. The van drove off before I had closed the door. I crawled my way forward to sit in the passenger's seat. The van was empty except for the driver. I lifted my goggles, pulled the face mask down, and turned to thank him for the ride. But before I could speak he glanced toward me and I gave a little gasp of recognition.

It was the Russian priest who had invited me to tea with the Metropolitan.

"Good morning," he said in his unaccented Russian.

"Good morning," I said in my best effort to imitate him. "And thank you for doing this."

"You are welcome," he said, "but thank me when we are outside the city. In the meantime, please sit low in the seat with your hood up."

I did as he asked and we drove quickly through the many rings of the city toward the open desert beyond. The direction we followed passed by the methane-oxygen refinery and the airport, taking a dirt road off the tarmac just as the sun broke the horizon. We bounced down the regolith road, winding our way deeper into the desert. The road was rough and seldom used. We did a kidney bounce for at least an hour until we came to a small hut tucked up under a ravine. The structure looked like a yurt, a squat circular building made of Mars bricks with a tent like roof of corrugated Martian steel. A single stove pipe poked its finger through the center of the building.

"This is a hermitage," said the priest, "We use it for private retreats. It is a place for meditation and prayer. No one comes here otherwise."

He stepped out of the van and walked toward the hermitage. I grabbed my bag out of the back and followed him. At the door I asked him, "Is this where I am to stay?"

"Only for a little while," he said, "In three days someone else will be coming to get you. You will know them."

"How will I know them?" I asked as we stepped inside, but the priest didn't answer.

He walked into the gloom and fired up an old lantern. Its yellow light exposed the interior of the hermitage. As it did so, it set fire to the gold and silver casings of a score of icons. They glittered like jewels in the soft light. Colored glass candle holders were suspended from the ceiling; votive lights hung before the images of Russian saints, of Jesus, and of the Theotokos. A low bench held incense, tattered prayer books and a Russian Bible, not the reed-paper type, but real paper books. Old and rare. The floor was covered with thick Persian rugs, rich in deep reds, blues and gold. The whole yurt was filled with the smell of frankincense and sandalwood. A single pot-bellied stove, heated by a methane-oxygen pump, sat in the center of the hermitage. An old samovar rested on a table next to it with glasses for tea lined up in their filigreed holders. There were packets of freeze dried soup, cheese and crackers, enough to get me through my three day vigil.

The priest lit one of the votive lights, crossed himself and muttered a prayer before the icon of Our Lady of Kiev. He touched the ground with his right hand and crossed himself again before starting to leave.

"You will be safe here for now," he said, "Perhaps you can find comfort in prayer."

"I will," I said, "and thank you again."

He only nodded. His black beard disguised any smile he may have offered me. He stepped through the door and closed it quietly behind him. I stood for a moment looking at the icons, then ran to the door.

"Please tell His Beatitude that I am grateful," I called to the priest.

The Russian waved his hand to show me he understood, stepped into the van, and drove off the way we had come. Already the Martian sun was turning the canyon walls to a dusty reddish orange. Streaks of shadow cut the desert floor like slices of a pie. I went back into the hermitage and closed the door. Only when I started to say my own prayer to God's Mother did I realize he had never told me how I would recognize who was coming to get me.

By my third day at the hermitage I was starting to get a little jumpy. I had run out of ways to blame myself for the disaster I had brought down on my friends and my church. With no one to talk to (Dr. Wu had kept my portable ComCom so I could not be traced and its signal would indicate I was still in Burroughs Base) I spent my days in the hermitage sleeping, worrying, and praying. In that order. Not that prayer is an afterthought with me. I have been praying all my life. I was praying even before I was religious. People in trouble are accustomed to spontaneous prayer. *Oh God, please get me out of this.* I had been saying that prayer since I was twelve. I am still saying it. That may account for why my piety is different from that of the other priests who have stayed in the hermitage. They probably haven't messed up as much in their lives. So their prayers are scheduled and organized. Mine are random. They pop up even when I least expect them.

In fact, I said one of these instant prayers when I heard a noise outside the yurt on the third day.

Oh God, don't let that be The Vegas.

I went to the door and eased it open. The wind had picked up. Outside dust eddies were swirling over the edges of the ravine. One of them had blown a tin can over the side. It had clattered against the rocks and caused me to jump. Where the can had come from, how far it had been blown over the desert, I had no idea. Maybe its fate was like mine. Just caught on the wind and tossed against the rocks.

I closed the door and tried some more intentional prayers. I lit all the votive candles in the hermitage. I sat on a cushion, looking at the faces of the saints. I prayed for Digby, wherever he was, for Theresa, Maria, Isidore, Beth and Kalisha, even for Ambrose who looked vaguely like one of the icons watching me pray. I prayed for all the people in the diocese, asking that they be safe. I prayed for Dr. Wu listening in his garden and for the Russian clergy who had helped me. I prayed for Clare, so far away on Earth and in such trouble, trouble I had caused. I prayed for myself, and was still praying, when I thought I heard something.

It wasn't another tin can. I knew that.

I got up. I went to the door. It was past twilight. The stars were beginning to blink on over the crest of the ravine. The air was cold enough to turn my breath into clouds. I squinted into the darkness, straining to see if anyone was out there. There was no sound except for the hiss of the lantern from inside the yurt.

I was about to turn and go back to my prayers when I caught a shape moving through the deep purple shadows. There was no mistake. Something out there was coming toward me. I considered going to find my night vision goggles, but was afraid to waste time looking for them. I suddenly realized that I was standing in a square of light in the doorway of the yurt. A perfect target. I stepped outside and closed the door behind me.

Whatever it was stopped.

I crouched down, straining my eyes into the night. I thought I could make out the black outline of a...of a what? It was like the bulk of a shadow with substance, something large and round, out of place in the sharp corners of the ravine. It wasn't moving now. Just standing there. Or was it? I felt my heart start to tap dance inside my chest. My mind was clicking through options, but nothing made sense for the thing in the night. It wasn't the silhouette of an ATV or a truck. It was too big to be human...way too big.

I stayed perfectly still and kept my eyes on it. Then, just as Diemos, Mars's second moon, rose over the desert floor, I saw two streamers of white breath drift from the dark shape and disappear. It was alive. It was something big. And it was watching me.

Oh God, I thought, I'm not dreaming. This is real. Something is out there.

Was it panic or purpose that sent me running back into the yurt? A bit of both to be honest. I darted inside and started looking around... for what? A weapon? I could feel my heart thudding against my chest. I was alone in the desert in a mud brick box with a monster outside. Nothing breathing on Mars could be, should be, as big as that shape in the night. It wasn't possible. But there it was. And I was alone in the night with it. My prayer life kicked into over drive.

Oh God, get me out of this and I promise to be good.

I fumbled around in the yurt looking for anything I could use to defend myself. Finally I grabbed the only large object I could find, a metal cross laying on the table beside the Russian prayer books. I picked it up, feeling its weight in my hand. It would have to do. I went to the door and pressed my ear against it, listening.

Silence.

I held my breath. Faintly, I heard something moving toward the hermitage. Rocks were shifting beneath the movement of feet. They were coming closer. I gripped the cross in my hand. I heard what sounded like a snort. Then silence again. Whatever it was, it was right outside.

What I did next makes no sense. Like all human beings I am that strange chemistry between fight and flight. The ancient adrenalin of survival took over and without thinking I lifted the cross, swung the door open and leaped outside, ready to do or die.

The sticky, rancid goo of a wad of thick snot hit me square in the face.

I sputtered, wiping the mess from my eyes. With strings of snot dripping from one hand and the cross dangling from the other, I looked up through the pale light coming out of the yurt into the face of the creature from the Martian night.

It was a camel.

"A Salaam 'Aleykum," said a voice.

I looked above the drooping face of the camel to see Alima Shariff pulling the hajib from her face. She was laughing.

"Are you ready to go?"

I rode through the rest of that night on a camel, swaying beneath the stars of the Martian sky. At first, it was awkward, but once I had settled into the gentle rocking motion it was very peaceful. Alima rode next to me. Her uncle, Kamil, rode just behind us. As our little caravan made its slow way through the trackless desert, Alima told me that Dr. Wu had contacted them and asked for their help in getting me out of harm's way.

"You know Dr. Wu?" I asked her.

"Very well," she said, "he helped us create our orchards at New Medina."

"But how did he get in touch with you?" I asked, "I thought we weren't supposed to use the ComCom."

"We didn't," she said, "The Vegas is sure to be monitoring as many links as they can. They would have learned of your escape. We use this." She patted a small box strapped to the saddle of her camel. "Short wave radio."

"I didn't think anyone used those anymore," I said.

"They don't," she said, "which is why we do. The Vegas will be watching the roads and airports, but not the open desert. New Medina will be the last place they will think to look. And just like you, they will not expect you to make your getaway by camel." She delivered those last words with a grin I could see clearly in the rosy mist of a Martian morning.

I gave her a sheepish but honest reply, "I knew there were camels on Mars," I said, "I just didn't expect this one. Or you, for that matter."

"They didn't tell you I would be your contact?"

"No. Maybe it was to keep you safe if The Vegas caught me before you got there."

Alima only nodded and we rode on until it got light. Her uncle guided us into a sheltered space within the shadows of a large crater.

"We will travel by night. Now we can make camp and rest out of sight," he explained, "just to be careful. This is sandstorm season so there are no flights to worry about, but still, never underestimate The Vegas."

He bedded the animals down under an outcropping of rock while Alima and I cooked up some breakfast on a small portable oxy-meth stove. We sat quietly watching the light break over the desert floor. In the distance a dust devil traced a finger of wind over the sand.

"When will we get to New Medina?" I asked.

"In two days," her uncle said, "Insha'Allah." God willing.

"If there are no storms," said Alima looking out into the pink sky, "It is Dragon Month. Not a good time to be out in the open desert."

"I am sorry to make you take that chance," I said, "It is not what I would have chosen to ask."

"Sometimes we are chosen without being asked," she said quietly.

"It is God's will," said her uncle as he stood up to unroll the sleeping bags.

Alima looked down at the hard red clay beneath our rock shelter. From the corner of the overhang I heard one of the camels shift its weight and complain with a sound that reminded me of a donkey bray.

"Tell me about New Medina," I said.

"Tonight," she replied, "right now I am going to sleep."

The three of us found as soft a spot as we could in different places under the lip of the overhang and crawled into our sleeping bags. At first I felt like the camel and wanted to complain about having to sleep on hard ground, but soon I was drifting into the warmth of the bag, leaving the wind to sweep the face of Mars as the distant sun rose to watch in silence.

Mary Magdalene was making breakfast. The Apostles were sleeping in the shade.

"Do you have to do all of the cooking?" I asked her.

"Most of it," she said, "but I don't mind."

"Because it is woman's work?" I asked.

She laughed.

"That's right, woman's work" she said, "just like writing down what Jesus says."

"Oh, I see. So you are like his secretary," I said.

Mary Magdalene laughed again as she flipped the eggs.

"Not exactly," she said, "More like his speech writer."

On the second evening of our night journey Alima told me about New Medina. It had been founded by refugees of the Muslim Diaspora, the Muhajirs, who had come to Mars seeking a new beginning for their faith. They chose to settle far out into the desert. Their goal, just as the goal of their first ancestors at old Medina, was to form a community according to the teachings of the Prophet. It was to be an oasis of peace in the midst of a hostile world.

New Medina had become that oasis, literally.

"With the help of Dr. Wu we found water under the regolith," she said, "We used it to irrigate our fields and become self-sufficient. We have developed new species of plants that can thrive in the changing eco-system of Mars. We even have engineered small date palms, fig trees, and olive groves. We have the first orchards on Mars. Perhaps, the first forests."

"A forest on Mars?"

"Yes," she said with a clear sense of pride in her voice, "you will see them when we come to New Medina."

"Insha'Allah," said Kamil from his place behind us as we rode through the night.

"We owe a great deal to Dr. Wu," said Alima, "but we also have taken his ideas and adapted them to our experience on Home World. You might say, we have become experts in survival. The Diaspora has made us so."

"I am sure it has," I said, "I know that your people have suffered a great deal."

I thought about the Drought and how it had cast the people of the Middle East and North Africa out into the dying world around them. Many had starved or been killed in the violence that preceded the order of the two Empires. Many more had scattered like seeds driven by a hot wind to find refuge wherever they could. Jerusalem, Cairo, Alexandria, Baghdad…all were gone. Only their survivors clung to the edges of the Med Marsh. The rest were lost on what was left of the Earth.

"But we have grown stronger too," she said, "Our faith has sustained us. Now we can make a new beginning."

"Here on Mars," I said looking at Alima's silhouette swaying against the map of stars that surrounded us.

"Yes," she said, "here on Mars."

With the coming of light we found our second hiding place. The Chryse Planitia is flatland desert, but near the great cone of the Sharonov crater buckled rock form ridges along the surface, dissected by the wadis of long vanished river beds. In these ravines are places gouged out by wind and sand storms, natural clefts in the hard stone walls where caves offer a shelter from the sun. We found a larger one for our patient camels and a smaller one for ourselves. After another simple meal of lentils and flat bread we drank tea and talked before we slept.

Kamil told me that by the next evening we should make New Medina. He said it was hidden in a valley in the Tempe Terra, a vast expanse of desert that leads to Olympus Mons, the highest mountain in the Solar System, over twice as high as Mount Everest.

"Imagine a Bedouin camp in a grove of olive trees beneath windmills bringing water through a network of small canals."

"You live in tents?" I had asked him.

"Many of us do," he said, "It is how we remain humble before God. We never forget that we are only the temporary keepers of the Garden of God."

"The sand storms don't blow your tents away?"

"We are in a canyon that protects us from the worst of the weather. It is our refuge."

"We say that we live in God's pocket," said Alima.

Kamil smiled. "That's what the children call it."

I carried the images of New Medina with me as I settled into my sleeping bag. I slept. I dreamed. Bedouin camps beside Martian canals. Camels wandering through forests beneath a mountain that reached Heaven. Windmills turning slow circles in a hidden valley. Eden, the pocket of God. Kamil, a man who looked like a prophet. Alima, a young woman who looked...who looked...

Alima's face vanished like the mists of Mars. I felt Kamil's hand shake me awake. I opened my eyes to see him pointing toward the sky. Alima was already crouching near us under the rocky overhang, a pair of binoculars pressed to her eyes.

"Mining drones," she said and pointed in the same direction as Kamil.

I quickly crawled out of my bag. It was already morning. The sun turned the desert a uniform shade of dirty orange. Objects were hard to make out in the haze, but I thought I could see what looked like a bird circling above the desert floor. Only there are no birds on Mars.

"It's a drone, alright," said Alima, "but what would it be doing out here in Dragon Month?"

"I don't think they are prospecting," her uncle replied, "at least not for rocks."

Alima and Kamil lay prone on the ground. I followed their example and kept watching the sky. At first I could only make out one bird shape, but then I saw the second one, crossing and re-crossing the desert floor in a zigzag pattern about two hundred meters in the air.

"What are mining drones?" I whispered to Kamil.

"Flying drills," he said quietly, "Remote spectrometers with lasers and blasting projectiles."

"Can they see us?"

"They can see our heat signature," he said.

"Or that of the camels," said Alima, looking over toward the animals that rested in the shade of the larger overhang. It was separated from us by at least ten meters of open sunlight. It was not as deep a shelter as ours and the camels were not wearing any covering as they knelt in the thin shadows.

Without speaking Kamil crawled back to his saddle and pulled out a rifle. The mining drones were now clearly zigzagging in our direction.

Suddenly both drones came to a full stop, hovering just beyond where we lay. I could see the sun glint off of their torpedo shaped bodies, sleek metal with dragonfly wings.

"Don't move," Kamil said, bringing the rifle up slowly.

We waited.

One of the drones seemed to turn in mid-air, pointing its nose toward the shelter where the camels were hunkered down, ignorant of the danger that was suspended above them. Kamil did not wait to see if what we all guessed was about to happen. He pulled the trigger and the crack of the rifle echoed through our shelter like a thunder clap.

The lead drone, the one that had targeted the camels, swiveled at an angle, one of its dragonfly wings spinning off toward the desert floor. As it spun sideways, a ribbon of red laser light flailed up toward the sky. The second drone pivoted in reaction, away from the camels and directly toward us. Before Kamil could get off another shot its projectile blast had exploded the rocks outside our hiding place into a fine red fog of vaporized rubble.

"Run," shouted Kamil.

I jumped to my feet.

Alima was scrambling back into the shelter. I heard Kamil fire off another round. A second explosion knocked me to the ground.

"This way," I heard Alima shout through the echo of sound and swirl of dust. I saw her moving in a crouch toward the camels, holding another rifle in her hand. I followed her. Just as we broke into the sunlight a third and final rifle shot rang out followed by a cry of pain. I looked back but could see nothing in the chaos of crumbling rock and billowing dust.

The camels were on their feet, trying to run but hobbled by the tethers we had used to keep them from wandering. As I bolted through the sunlight I heard another snake-like hiss as a laser hit the sand where I had been running. Alima was standing just in the shadow of the larger cave.

"The camels," she shouted, "don't let them break their legs."

I saw her bring the gun to her shoulder. I jumped between the bucking camels fumbling to get a hold on the ropes that bound them. I heard a rifle shot. Another explosion and what sounded like a yelp of pain. I frantically pulled at the ropes. The first camel suddenly came free and charged out of the shelter. The second and third followed it, galloping off in a blind panic. The drone was still in the air. It turned its nose toward them. In a second its laser had sliced through one of the poor animals and left it lying in a black pool of blood. The drone swung to target the other two camels but never got the chance. From behind me I heard Alima fire one more round. The drone shattered into pieces, its wings folding in as it plummeted to the rocks below.

I turned to see Alima slump to the ground. As I ran toward her I could see the two camels running into the distance. I lifted her up. Her hajib was covered in blood. Her face lifeless beneath a shroud of red dust.

CHAPTER NINE

Uncle Kamil was dead. Alima and I buried him beneath a grave of stones, each of us praying for him in our own way. She was hurt. She had been hit by a flying piece of rock blasted by the last mining drone before she could destroy it. Beneath her hajib her hair was matted with blood, but the cut was only superficial. As for me, I was filled with regret. I had no idea how The Vegas had found me, but I knew I was a target for their brand of problem solving.

I felt responsible for Kamil's death. I felt responsible for stranding Alima in the desert, injured and alone with a hunted man. I had stupidly released the camels because I did not know what I was doing.

Back home, in Pilgrim's Playground, I was a tough guy. I knew the streets and I knew the score. But on Mars I was nothing but a walking liability. I had brought The Vegas down on my friends. I had put my diocese in jeopardy and probably wrecked the church for Ima Clare. I had endangered Dr. Wu and implicated the Russians. Now I was visiting disaster on Alima and her people. Some tough guy.

"I am so sorry," I had said to Alima, "I never meant for any of this to happen."

"I know," was all she said.

We packed up what we could carry and started walking. We knew that The Vegas drones might be back. If we stayed put we would be a stationary target. We had to risk the walk and hope that we would see them before they saw us.

"They will expect us to head straight for New Medina," she said, "so we will go another way. It will be longer, but it may be safer."

Rather than make the crossing over the Tempe Terra to the east, we turned north, climbing up the edges of the Sharonov to a mesa above the desert floor. It was a hard scramble and we were both winded when we made it to the top. Before we tried to cross the mesa I scanned the skies for any signs of drones while Alima tried the short wave to warn New Medina about what had happened.

Communications on Mars depends on the ComCom satellites that ring the planet. The only interruption is during sand storms when the entire planet can be blanketed by winds just shy of hurricane force. In the first years of settlement, before the satellites, prospectors and terraformers had used short wave radio. It worked, but the range was limited. As we huddled down on the rim of the plateau our hope was that we were close enough to New Medina to get through.

Alima called in several times, but only once did she hear a crackling response. New Medina was still more than a day's hike from our location. Close enough, but if the weather was bad over the valley where the Muhajirs made their home they might not pick up the signal. Or if they did, they might not be able to reply. Alima made the effort anyway. She explained that we had been attacked. She told them that Kamil was dead and that we were moving north to avoid the drones. Most of all, she warned them about The Vegas and told them to be alert for any reprisals.

"Do you think they heard us?" I asked as we packed up the radio.

"God willing," she said, "but I can't be sure."

I could tell by the expression on her face that she was worried. The image of Vegas drones blasting the tents and orchards of New Medina hung between us like an unspoken mirage of fear. Some tough guy, I thought again. Now I may have brought the apocalypse of The Vegas down on a peaceful village of scientist farmers. I tried to shake the feeling off as I followed Alima out onto the escarpment, but it stayed with me like my shadow, a moving stain on the desert as we walked in the late morning sun.

We rarely spoke to one another as we covered the desolate kilometers across the Martian mesa. I think we were both aware that we were open targets, like bugs walking across a kitchen floor. If someone saw us from above we would be easy to step on. We walked at a steady pace in the thin air. We kept our eyes either on the ground before us, or on the skies behind us. Several times we stopped to scan the horizon with the binoculars, but we saw nothing. We walked on.

As the sun began its arc downward to the far side of Mars the wind picked up, spitting dust against our goggles. I could taste the dirt as it coated my lips like salt. The far end of the mesa was lost in a fog of swirling sand eddies, spinning like cones of silt through the air. Dragon Month had begun to move across the face of Mars.

"We have to hurry," she said, pulling her face mask up against the wind.

"Is it a sand storm?" I asked, but she shook her head.

"No, not a storm. You will see it if it comes. But we need to get off this flat ground."

She turned and began walking quickly. I kept pace, the wind pushing me back with an insistent hand. I am in good shape for a guy in his fifties, and taller than Alima by at least three inches, but I was hard pressed to keep up with her. I felt a cold sweat coat my skin beneath my overalls. My mouth was dry but whether from thirst or nerves I couldn't tell. All I knew was that I was determined not to be a problem for the woman who walked beside me.

By the time the Martian twilight was turning the sky from pink to lavender I could begin to see the outline of another canyon in the distance. The flat line of the horizon looked broken. Jagged edges of higher ground appeared in the gathering shadows of evening. In less than a kilometer we would come to another ancient Martian waterway, a deep ravine scoured out by a flood over three billion years before. It would give us some safety from the wind that continued to pelt us with a fine rain of sand and rock. I had been walking slightly ahead of Alima when I saw the edge of the mesa. I turned to ask if she saw it too. Her head was down, bent against the wind, but I did not speak to her. Instead, I stopped and stood still. Over her shoulder, half a kilometer away, a mining drone sent two beams of light through the dust, searching the floor for bugs to step on.

In Pilgrim's Playground there is a museum of sorts. It is not a museum of paintings or sculpture since The Vegas is not noted for its appreciation of the fine arts. It is a freak show museum, a collection of the lurid, the bizarre, the titillating. A stuffed two headed sheep. The holo image of a man with multiple piercings over his whole body. A torture cage from old Europe with spikes drawing fake blood from a mannequin. I had gone to this museum when I was a teenager. I walked past all of the exhibits without batting an eye, except for one thing.

In a corner of the museum was a small glass case. Hunched inside was a child. She was an Inca child, brought to the mountain top to be sacrificed to gods long forgotten. She had died of exposure, high on the Andes, frozen into a mummy that would always huddle against the cold, seeking a warmth it could never find.

I thought about her because I felt like her.

Alima and I were huddled into a small space, hugging our knees in an effort to stay hidden, shivering from cold. The wind was howling around the rim of the canyon like a dragon. Two red searchlights continued to probe around us, looking for a sacrifice.

This mining drone was larger than the other models. It was sturdy enough to stay aloft even in a strong wind. It was sure to pack a heavier punch as well.

When I yelled at Alima to run the drone was still half a kilometer away, but it was fast. Too far and too fast to try shooting it down. By the time we ran to the drop off into the ravine, it was almost directly over us. It had registered our heat signature. It was targeting in for the kill.

If there is a God, and it's my job to believe there is, one proof must be in the fact that we jumped down to find a small burrow on the ledge where we landed. Otherwise we would have been trying to scramble down sliding rocks in plain sight of the drone as it swooped over the lip of the plateau. Even in the dust swirls and the fading light, it could have picked us off easily.

I could feel Alima shivering next to me. Our little hole in the ground was a permafrost box.

"If it doesn't leave soon," she whispered, "we will start to freeze."

The Martian night is not what it used to be. When the first settlers arrived the night temperature could drop to -120F or lower. Now, after a century of pumping greenhouse gases into the atmosphere, it can stay a balmy -10F. Cold enough to turn you into an Inca mummy, but survivable if you are wearing the right equipment. We had the right equipment but could not put it on until we could stand. And we couldn't stand until the drone decided we were an anomaly and went off in search of better targets.

I leaned sideways, still holding my knees, and peeked out with one eye around the opening to our shelter. I had seen the glow of the red lights sweep over the entrance a few minutes before, but Alima was right, if we didn't get out of the burrow soon we would be sacrifices to the dark gods of The Vegas.

I did not see any lights. I unfolded and poked my head out further. The drone was moving away now, up the canyon, its lights crisscrossing the canyon walls in the darkness.

"It's gone," I said, "let's get out of here before it comes back."

We painfully straightened ourselves out of the burrow and quickly covered ourselves in thermal overalls. While we had lost almost all the other equipment, including most of our water, to the earlier drone attack, at least the thermal gear had survived. Without it we would be dead.

We flipped on our night vision goggles and moved down the canyon wall, looking for a better place to hide. The warmth inside the suit began to unstiffen my joints and my muscles started to work again as Alima and I helped one another down the ravine. We had to take care not to rip our suits in the process, but we went as fast as we could in the event our red eyed friend decided to turn around.

The wind was stronger now. It was gusting at 40 to 50km bursts, slapping us around as we found the canyon floor. The canyon was a wind tunnel, funneling the air out toward the desert. The dust pelted our goggles. Alima reached out and took my hand.

"Stay together," she shouted, "and follow my lead."

Like a couple of Inca kids escaping sacrifice we inched our way hand-in-hand through the green light of our night vision, always glancing back and up to make sure the drone was still out of sight. We had probably gone about a kilometer or more when our visibility started to reach a critical level. Alima put her face close to mine and shouted over the wind.

"There used to be a mining camp here," she said, "Keep an eye out for any shape that looks square."

We moved through the green fog, tripping over rocks. I held her hand tightly, afraid that if I let go I might not find her again. The pack on my back felt heavier with each step, the dirt clogging my nose turned into sandpaper. My spontaneous prayer life was up and running. I had been saying a litany of thanks while crouched in the burrow. Now I was back to asking for more help.

And help came.

"There!" I heard her cry out and she started to pull me forward. I looked ahead to make out a square shape becoming more distinct as it emerged through the haze of night sand. It was a brick hut. A single, small brick hut sitting in the darkness, but to me, at that moment, it was the most beautiful thing I had ever seen. We found the metal door and pushed it open. Sand had drifted into small dunes around the hut but inside it was still intact. I shoved the door closed against the wind and turned to see Alima moving through the darkness, fumbling through the clutter of the abandoned cabin. She found a lantern.

"Cover the windows," she said with a voice that seemed as tired as she looked.

I helped her cover the two small windows of the miner's hut, making sure no light could escape to draw the attention of the drone. We sat in its dim light sharing a sip of water from the only bottle we had left. Alima wiped a bare hand over her dust caked face. Her eyes were red. Her nose raw. She looked exhausted. When I spoke, my breath turned to fog in the cold air.

"Thank God we made it," I said.

"I have been," she said. Her eyes met mine. She smiled.

It was then that I first thought how beautiful she was, but I left the thought unspoken as the wind rattled the world around us.

I was sitting inside the whale with Jonah. It was damp and cold. I was thirsty but there was nothing to drink.

"Well tough guy," he said, "what brought you here?"

"I screwed everything up," I said, "I'm bad luck."

"I don't believe in luck," said Jonah, "Things just happen."

"You don't think we have a destiny?"

"Oh sure," he said, "We have a destiny,"

"To do God's will?"

"No, to screw things up."

"So God is not before us planning our future?"

Jonah shook his head and laughed.

"No," he said, "God is behind us cleaning up our past."

"We're almost out of water."

I had been standing by the window watching the dust fly around in the wind. We had been in the miner's hut for two days. The wind had grown stronger. I turned to see Alima holding up the water bottle. It was almost empty.

"More bad luck," I said.

"I didn't think Christians believed in luck," she said shaking the bottle at me with a smile.

"I guess I'm just superstitious," I said, "It was good luck to find this place. Bad luck to not have found any water here."

"It is God's will," she said, "Luck is just a name we give to what we can't control."

"Well, I must be the luckiest guy on Mars," I said, "since apparently I am not in control of much of anything."

She laughed. It was a gentle laugh. The kind that comes easily from a soul that is at rest enough to have no need to be guarded.

"You are so funny," she said, "Not at all what I expected."

We looked at one another for a moment. Each of us smiling. But, as usual for me, I found the intimacy of eye contact a little more than I could handle so I looked away, out toward the storm.

"How long do you think this storm will last?" I asked.

Alima shook her head.

"Hard to say. It is still early in Dragon Month. It could blow itself out at any time. Or it could last for two weeks." She sat the bottle down and looked at me.

"Well, at least we don't have to worry about drones, not in this weather."

"True," she said, "but if we don't get out of here soon they won't have to worry about us either."

I crossed the room to sit down. She had spread our supplies out on a small table. We had a few more packets of MAC meals, the kind the military on Home World issues to soldiers in the field. There was the rifle. Our thermal gear. The short wave radio. It was useless to try to contact New Medina in the sand storm.

"I really am sorry I got you into this," I said, "Whether you believe in luck or not, I seem to have only brought you trouble and loss."

"It was God's will," she said, hugging her arms around herself against the chill of the cabin.

"I don't think we should blame God for my stupid mistakes."

Alima turned to look at me.

"What you did was not stupid," she said, "It was courageous."

I sat down across from her. Outside the wind shrieked as it threw more sand against our hideout.

"Sometimes there is a fine line between courage and stupidity," I said, "I'm not always sure which side of that line I am on."

"You stood up to evil," she said firmly, "You tried to stop The Vegas from infecting Mars. You risked your life to keep our world free from that evil. I would call that courage."

"Is that why you agreed to help me? Because I was trying to stop The Vegas?"

Alima rubbed her eyes with one hand.

"When Dr. Wu told us what you had done and asked us to hide you, we knew it was risky. But we decided it was also right. We do not want The Vegas here anymore than you do. Any more than the Russian Church does. On that, we all agree. So, yes, we agreed to help you, but by doing that, we also were helping what you stood for."

Her words hit me, but I tried not to flinch.

What I stood for.

And what was that? I was an ex-Zappie, an addict pretending to be holy, a leader who had only brought his people into deeper trouble. I had gotten Alima's uncle killed. What exactly did I stand for?

"You are courageous," said Alima again, "I am glad we helped you.

Otherwise, my uncle's death would have no meaning."

I looked back at her. Her face seemed drawn and somehow much older.

"Your uncle was the courageous one," I said, "He died doing what he thought was right. He gave his life to save mine. He did it to help his people. That is a courage I will never have, Alima. I am so grateful to him…to you…for all that you have done for me. I have no words to say how much."

We looked at one another through the hazy half-light of the miner's hut. Finally she spoke in a hushed voice.

"My uncle did the will of God," she said with a voice on the edge of breaking, "through his life…and through his death. He believed in what you were doing. So do I." A single tear ran down her dust streaked face. She wiped it away.

I did not know what else to say. Only twice in my life had anyone said they believed in me. Clare. Now Alima. Both had set me on a journey.

I stood up and went to the window.

"Why do you blame yourself so much?" she asked from behind me, "I thought Christians believed they could always be forgiven."

"We do," I said turning toward her, "it's just sometimes hard for us…hard for me… to remember that."

Alima smiled. It made her seem so beautiful.

"Maybe that is why God put us together, so I could remind you."

"That I am forgiven?"

"Yes, I think so," she said still smiling, "and that you are a courageous man, in spite of yourself."

"Well, if your job is to remind me I am forgiven for my shortcomings, trust me, you will get a lot of practice."

I smiled back at her.

"You are so not what I expected," she said.

I was going to ask her if that was a good thing or a bad thing, but she got up to find a blanket to wrap around herself. She pulled it over her shoulders and huddled up on the bunk in the corner of the small cabin. The little oxy-meth heater was doing its best to warm the room, but it still felt cold. For a moment, I thought of sitting next to her. I thought of putting my arms around her. But I hesitated. And in that hesitation the impulse was lost, drifting down into the dark sea of regret.

Why do you blame yourself so much?

"We've got to get out of here soon," I said looking out into the storm.

"We have one more day of water," I heard her say in a sleepy voice, but that wasn't what I had been thinking about.

The next morning the wind had stopped. I was sleeping on the floor, hunched up in my thermals. I opened my eyes to hear the strange sound of nothing. No wind beating at the windows or rattling the door. Just nothing.

"Alima," I called in a hoarse voice. "Alima".

She sat up on the bed across the room.

"Listen," I said.

She rubbed her eyes, cocking her head like a small puppy, and then she grinned.

"It's stopped," she said.

"We can get out of here," I smiled.

She jumped off the bed.

"Let's go," she said, "We have to make New Medina before the storm comes back."

I was on my feet. "Or the drones."

We packed up our few supplies and went for the door.

"Grab that drill," she said pointing to a corkscrew shaft leaning against the corner, "We may need it."

"I don't think we have much time for prospecting," I said feeling the weight of the drill. It wasn't large, but it would be a fair weight to carry over a long distance.

"Are you thirsty?" she asked opening the door. A small pile of sand collapsed onto the floor by her feet.

I nodded.

"Then bring it," she said, stepping outside. I hefted the drill over my shoulder and followed her out into the clear light of the desert.

We walked quickly toward the mouth of the canyon. I think we were both so glad to be out of the miner's hut that we had more energy than our dehydrated bodies might have expected. The sun felt warm after shivering inside a box for days. The air was fresh. The canyon walls opened like a hand spilling us out into the red sand of the valley before us.

I didn't ask if Alima knew the way. I knew she did. She was born into this place. She had a mental map imprinted in her memory from years of growing up in the desert. I just kept walking beside her, scanning the sky for any sign of mining drones. We hugged the curving wall of the Sharonov for about five kilometers before we stopped and knelt down looking out into the open desert of the Tempe Terra. Alima cranked up her short wave and tried another call but we still got no response. We had walked farther from the settlement during our run across the Martian mesa. The chances that they would hear us were less likely now than before.

Alima pointed toward some distant hills. They were at least fifty kilometers away. Maybe more. The barren surface of Mars shimmered before us in the rusty light of noonday.

"We have to cross here to get to New Medina," she said.

"How far?" I asked.

"A day. A little more. Unless the storm comes back."

"Then what?" I asked.

Alima looked at me.

"Then we are in trouble. To be caught out in the open in a

sandstorm is not a good thing. Especially without water. If it blew for very long we would be lost and die of thirst."

"What other choice do we have?" I asked with a shrug, "If we stay put The Vegas will find us. They can't miss that miner's cabin in the clear light of day. They will blast it just to make sure we aren't hiding in it."

"That's my guess too," she said, "and I don't know if any of my people will be looking for us. I don't know if they heard my first transmission. They may think we have stayed put near Burroughs Base to avoid the storms."

"So we have to risk it," I said, "But why do we have to carry this thing? Its heavy and it will only slow us down."

"There's a dry lake out there," said Alima, "If we are lucky, it will have water."

She hefted the drill over her shoulder.

"I thought you didn't believe in luck," I smiled.

"Bad choice of words," she said, "You are not a good influence on me."

We stood up, took a last look at the sky, and walked out onto the rough back of Mars. We walked toward the distant hills, stopping only occasionally to sweep the sky with binoculars. There was no sign of drones or of storms. Alima had told me that a sand storm looks like a wall of red dust moving over the horizon. A tsunami of sand, sweeping over the desert, at times, over the whole planet. Martian sand storms have been known to last for days. Even with the change in the climate from the oxy-makers and the greening of some areas in the northern hemisphere of Mars, the sand storms are a constant threat in the Martian winter.

Shortly after midday Alima pointed to a low ridge on the desert floor. "The lake bed is just ahead. We will search for water there."

"Good," I said through cracked lips, "This thing is getting heavy."

We walked another kilometer over rocky terrain until we came to a broad crater in the Martian regolith, not an impact crater since most of those are in the south, but a deep defile in the hard surface, the evidence of an ancient lake long gone in the drying of the distant past. Alima led us down into the lake bed.

"I'm going to look for water," she said, "You keep an eye out for drones."

I followed her orders and kept my eyes scanning the sky for any hint of drones. She began walking in a grid around the floor of the dry lake. From time to time she would stop and dig her heel into the crust of Martian regolith.

"What are you doing?" I called to her.

Alima was intently studying the rocky ground.

"Looking for any signs that there may be pockets of water forming beneath the surface," she called back to me. "There may be water trapped under the crust. If there is, the crust will be a slightly different texture. Now keep still and watch for drones."

I put the binoculars back up to my eyes and swept the horizon. Some thin wisps of cirrus clouds drifted through the pink afternoon light, but no sign of anything flying. Suddenly Alima gave a shout.

"Here," she yelled, "Bring the drill."

I hustled over to her, manhandling the drill in my arms.

"Try it here," she said.

I put the top of the corkscrew on the hard surface of the lake bed and fired up the motor. It began biting into the regolith.

"Hold it steady," she said over the sound of the motor.

I pushed down on the handle bars of the drill and felt it begin to dig its way through the crust. It bucked like the jackhammers I had seen on the streets of Pilgrim's Playground when I was a kid, watching the road crews chew up the tarmac. This was much quieter but it was the same idea. The corkscrew dug its way down into the Martian soil until the handle bars were almost to the surface. I put on the reverse and pulled it out.

We looked down into the post hole made by the drill. Nothing.

Alima gave no sign that she was disappointed. She just started walking again until she found another spot. We repeated the drilling. Again, we came up dry.

"I'm going to move further out," she said, "Just rest a minute."

She continued her sweep until she had another spot we could try. I hauled the drill over and we bored another well. This time, it worked. At first, the Martian clay seemed to darken. Then the moisture spread like a stain as the dry clay sucked up the water. Finally it rose through the post hole to become a tiny pool. Water, red from the iron of the soil, but water that could be purified and used. We had struck something much better than gold.

"You are brilliant," I exclaimed as we watched the water bubbling up by our feet.

Alima wiped her brow.

"Thank you," she said with a beautiful smile, "for not saying it was luck."

We filled our water bottles through filters, standard issue on any Martian canteen. I took a drink. It was like drinking medicine, but it was water and that was all I cared about. Alima and I sat down by our little oasis and rested. A slight breeze moved over us like a reward.

"We will have to find a place to stop by nightfall," she said.

I looked over my shoulder.

"The hills are still a long hike," I said, "We will have to find something out in the open."

Alima nodded.

"Not much in the way of shelter," she said, "But at least we won't die of thirst."

"Do we have to carry the drill anymore?" I asked.

Alima shook her head, "No, I think we can take our chances between here and New Medina."

We ate a packet of MAC meals and started our walk again. Without the load of the drill and with a stomach full of food and water I felt a burst of energy. I was chattering away to her with questions about the orchards at New Medina. She must have felt better too because she seemed much more relaxed. I even began to think that she was enjoying talking to me. We were day dreaming our way over the desert, talking about the future forests of Mars. We were laughing about Martian forest rangers riding through the trees on their camels. We were doing everything but watching the skies.

Which is why we never saw the wall of sand rising up behind us.

Chapter Ten

A Martian sand storm moves with the force of a tropical storm. It can clock wind speeds up to 70 or 80 kilometers an hour. It sand blasts everything in its path. At the moment Alima and I turned to look, we were in its path. There was no chance to out run the billowing wall that rose up behind us like a tidal wave. We had to find shelter. And fast.

I am no expert in the desert, but I am an expert in dodging a bullet. More than once in Pilgrim's Playground I had made it through another day by thinking fast enough on my feet to find a hole in the wall. Quickly scanning around us as we stood in the open desert I made the same kind of split second decision.

"This way!" I shouted. Grabbing her hand I ran for one of the larger rocks that sat on the desert floor. She didn't hesitate. We ran for the shelter of the rock and slid in behind it, our backs pressed against its solid surface. The blast of sand swallowed us. Like a white water river, it crashed with incredible force over and around the rock that protected us. Even with goggles on, we could barely see one another. Our masks covered our faces, but breathing was labored through the fine particles of wind-borne silt that swirled around us. There was nothing we could do but ride it out and pray.

Alima had said that a Martian storm can last for days. I knew that was true. On my way to Mars I had been given all of the usual background information for immigrants. I had heard about sand traps, radiation exposure, oxygen deprivation, and above all, about sand storms. The longest on record had lasted for two months, blanketing the entire surface of the planet. Sand storms had killed many of the First Settlers. But now, with early warning and buildings designed to withstand the winds, most Martians are able to cope. ATV trucks can plow through the storms and Martian homes are designed to function with emergency power if necessary. Air travel is curtailed, but otherwise life can continue without interruption. In fact, most Martians are proud to be hardy enough to take the storms in stride. Only out on the open desert is there still a real risk of dying. You can be buried alive. You can dehydrate. You can get lost never to be found. Those options gave me a lot to think about as I huddled next to Alima in the storm.

Religion is all about death.

As I sat in a swirl of red dust, I thought about something Elder Michael had taught us years before at the Farm. He had shown us a holopix of an ancient burial. A skeleton squeezed into a fetal position lying in sand, the faint traces of flowers still visible, the bones stained by red ochre. Red bones in red dust. A burial 100,000 years old.

Elder Michael said these burials were proof that humanity had come to religious consciousness by confronting death. Human beings no longer walked off and left their dead to be food for scavengers. They put them in graves and covered them with flowers and with red ochre. In doing so they crossed a bridge from being driven by instinct to being pulled by spiritual curiosity. They became aware. They began the journey of wonder toward faith. They asked questions about the meaning and value of life that we are still asking today. They invented religion as an answer.

Faith was born in dust and flowers.

I looked down at my hands and legs. I was covered in red ochre. The sand of Mars was sprinkled over me as if I was hunched up in my grave. I was sitting next to life, next to Alima, but I was under the shadow of death. I was in a sightless world, lost somewhere between the hard reality of the rock behind my back and an unknown future before my eyes. I had no power to save myself and no guess as to what might happen next. I was as anonymous as an ancient burial, but as real as the bones we share. All I had was faith that somehow it made sense or would make sense. The rest was just a storm.

I reached over and took hold of Alima's hand. She turned toward me. All I could see was her face mask, her eyes dimly showing through her goggles. She squeezed my hand.

Was it a hand like hers that first tossed flowers in a grave?

Was it a woman who set us on the path to religion? Yes, I thought, it very well could have been. A woman who first believed we were more than an accident. A woman grieving the loss of her baby. A woman who lost her child, her parent, her lover. She had seen death, seen it in a new way, and refused to give it the final word over her life, over any life. She had begun to dig in the hard ground, dig a nest for life. She had placed the body there, amid the flowers and the red ochre. Others had watched. And learned. And another great spiral of our history as human beings had begun to spin out into the stars.

Religion was born in dust and flowers. It was born in the heart of grief. It was born of a woman.

I huddled closer to Alima. With our heads pressed near I could hear her reciting a prayer in the language of her holy book, the Koran. I joined her in making my own prayers. Different words, different faiths, different people. But sitting together by that rock, covered in red sand, we were children of the same mother, even if we would never know her name.

The dawn came in silence. The pink eye of the sun peeped over the Martian mesas to find the red world at rest. The storm had passed.

When I awoke I saw Alima standing beside the rock, searching the sky with her binoculars.

"Good morning," I said, "Any sign of trouble?"

She brought the binoculars down and stretched. She was covered with a fine powder of sand. She looked like a ghost wearing a headscarf.

"I don't think anything is flying now," she said, "It's too unpredictable. Let's get moving and try to get to New Medina as quickly as we can."

We sat off at a fast pace. Even if we were both true believers, I don't think either of us wanted to tempt fate with another sand storm. We walked toward the hills before us. We did not stop to rest or eat. We just kept moving. It wasn't something we decided. It was just something we did. By nightfall we were at the base of the hills that climbed higher into the small mountain range that bordered the valley where New Medina sat in its shelter between the arms of a wide canyon. It was getting too dark to try to go any further so we found a cove of rocks and made a camp for the night. We ate the last of our MAC meals and drank some of the water. It still tasted like medicine but we didn't care. We were safe. We were off the desert floor and soon we would be at New Medina.

"I bet you will be glad to be home," I said leaning back to look at the Martian night.

Alima dusted her hands off and took a drink of water.

"I only hope there is a home to go to," she said quietly.

I rolled over to look at her. We had snapped one of the small glow packs that come with the thermal gear we were wearing. It gave us just enough light to see one another. What I saw was worry on her face.

"I don't think even The Vegas could get away with attacking a whole settlement," I said, "They can send up a few mining drones to hunt for us, but they wouldn't try to attack New Medina."

"Maybe," she said.

I remembered the image of burning orchards that had crossed my mind back on the mesa. I sat up and tried to sound as confident as I could.

"It's me that they want," I said, "and they're not stupid. If they go charging in to New Medina they will force the government to react. The Mars Central Authority might look the other way if a single troublemaker disappears in the desert, but they won't ignore anything on the scale of a whole town being hit."

Alima looked at me with an intense expression etched over her face.

"But we are very isolated," she said, "and very small. How would anyone know? Why would anyone care?" She looked back into the night sky. "We are Muslims," she said, "Why would anyone care?"

"I would care. Dr. Wu would care. The Russians would care. There are a lot of people who care, Alima."

Alima kicked at the sand with one foot and rubbed her eyes.

"I guess so," she said, "It is just hard to stop worrying."

"I understand," I said.

Alima looked at me again through the dim light of the glow pack.

"And I miss my uncle," she said in a small voice. I could see her eyes glisten in the faint light.

"I can only imagine," I said, "I am so sorry. But he died loving you and defending you. And that love will go on."

Alima nodded slowly.

"Yes," she said, "It will go on in Paradise."

The word caught me by surprise. I sat quietly for a moment. Beyond the pool of light in which we huddled the Martian desert stretched out beneath the starry sky. It was cold and quiet. An empty world with only silent rocks to keep the secret of its ancient past.

"Do you ever wonder what Heaven will be like?" I asked.

Alima wiped her eyes and gave me a tentative smile.

"Sometimes."

"I think it will be a big beach."

"A what?"

"A big beach," I said, "by the ocean. When I was a kid I always wanted to go to the beach. Pilgrim's Palace is near the ocean, but I rarely ever got to see it."

"I have no idea what you are talking about," laughed Alima, "I can't even imagine what an ocean must be like."

I smiled back.

"Well, that's why it will be Paradise," I said.

Alima laid back and cupped the back of her head in her hands. She looked up at the stars.

"Water as far as the eye can see," she sighed, "I hope you are right. I think I would like the beach."

I laid down beside her to look up into the Martian heavens. We were both quiet. Soon I could hear the rhythm of her breathing falling into sleep.

My eyes closed. The sand was still warm beneath my body. It felt like the beach. Just before I drifted into sleep I thought I could hear the sound of the ocean. An ancient echo from the lost seas of Mars.

The first thing I saw of New Medina was smoke rising from the valley. I was immediately anxious, but Alima said not to worry. There was a kiln for making pottery that sometimes gave off smoke. She had chosen not to call ahead on her short wave just to make sure there were no unexpected visitors listening in. We approached the valley cautiously, but before we were very near a single rider on a camel came tearing across the sand toward us, silent, but waving his arms. Alima squinted toward the rider and then smiled at me.

"It's my little cousin, Yusuf," she said, "He must have been watching for us."

The young boy galloped up to us. He tapped his camel down to a kneeling position, slid off, and hugged Alima with kisses on both cheeks.

"I was so worried," he kept saying, "I am so glad you are alright."
Alima tried to introduce me to him but the boy was too excited to
do more than glance at me with a quick nod of his head.

"We got most of your transmission," he said as we started walking
back toward the valley. Yusuf led the camel as he walked beside us.
"We heard the news about uncle Kamil," he said in a somber tone, "We
have been praying for him ever since. And for you. We thought you
were killed in the sand storm."

"We survived, thanks be to God," said Alima.

"Thanks be to God," repeated Yusuf, "But there is still trouble
waiting. That's why I watched for you. You must be very careful what
you say."

Alima grabbed the boy by his arm.

"What kind of trouble? Are there strangers in the town?"

Yusuf shook his head, his dark curls bouncing above his face.

"Not strangers," he said, "MACs. They have been waiting for the
bishop." Yusuf looked toward me.

"How did they know I would be here?"

"I don't know," Yusuf answered, "but I heard one of my cousins
say that the people who attacked you with the drones must have figured
out where you were going. They must have told the MACs."

We entered the valley of New Medina. It was very much as I had
imagined. Bright green fields made a checkerboard against the red soil
of Mars. The fields are separated by blue ribbons of water, an intricate
system of irrigation canals, not unlike those imagined by astronomers
on Earth when they first began to observe Mars through their
telescopes. In those days the rift valleys and ancient river beds that
crisscross the planet looked like canals. Astronomers like Percival
Lowell had believed they were manmade canals, created by a dying
Martian civilization to bring water down from the ice capped poles.
They were wrong, of course, but here, sustaining a Martian culture they
could never have envisioned, are real canals bringing new life to the

planet.

Tall windmills stand along the valley floor, turning slowly in the late morning breeze, their arms outstretched to hold sails of white canvas on metal rods that can be collapsed in a sand storm. There are several barn-like buildings made of Mars brick and fenced in yards where camels stood watching us pass by with lazy liquid eyes.

But the most distinctive feature of the settlement is Bedouin-style tents, nestled under small palm trees. They give New Medina the true appearance of an oasis in the Martian desert. An oasis of orchards. Beyond a row of tents I saw lines of small trees, standing with fingers raised to the sky, gnarled like hands with swollen joints, heavy from holding up their fruit. These are the orchards Alima had described. Hardy, squat little trees standing bravely against the red rock walls of the canyon. They are enclosed in low stone walls, row after row, reaching back into the valley.

"Olives," said Alima as we passed into the village, "there are fruit trees and dates too."

I wanted to ask about those, but by now we were being surrounded by Muhajirs, men and women dressed in the usual Martian overalls, all speaking at once, reaching out to embrace Alima. Some spoke an A'Salaam to me but most just looked at me with curiosity. How much of the story did they know? I couldn't tell by their expressions but they were obviously overjoyed to see Alima.

We were led through more clusters of tents and barns, with more fields flanking each side of the settlement under the watchful eye of their windmills, until we came to the center of the community, the large mosque that stood at the heart of New Medina. It was the same Roman-arch design so common to Martian architecture, rose colored, with Arabic lettering in a geometric design framing twin doors that led into the interior. Two tall minarets stood sentinel on each side of the mosque, each topped with a golden crescent. I could see the tiny balconies on the top of the minarets where the muezzin would call the faithful to prayer.

As soon as we came into the plaza before the mosque I saw three MAC vans parked outside. As we approached one of the MACs standing by the trucks hurried inside, returning in a moment with an officer in MAC uniform accompanied by two older Muhajirs.

The officer was a Chinese woman of middle age with short cropped hair and a broad face. She wore the regulation black overalls with a firearm strapped to her waist. Her voice was without inflection, but spoken in Chinese with a Martian accent.

"Are you Bishop Anthony?" she asked without introduction.

The crowd that had followed us was so quiet I could hear the creaking of the windmills. Yusuf stood beside Alima who was looking intently at the officer. I could see that he was holding her by the hand.

"Yes," I said, clearing my dry throat, "I am."

The officer did not change her expression which was no expression at all.

"Bishop Anthony," she said, "you are under arrest by order of the Mars Central Authority. You will accompany us back to Burroughs Base."

"Under arrest?" exclaimed Alima, "What for?" She looked to the two older Muhajirs but they remained stoic behind weather creased faces and white beards.

"The charge is complicity in subversion of the social order and evasion of arrest. Both are felony charges."

"Evasion of arrest?" I said, "I have been running for my life because The Vegas have been trying to kill me."

"You can tell that to the Magistrate."

"But he did not have anything to do with the riot," cried Alima, "What he says is the truth."

The officer ignored Alima and fixed her eyes on me. Her hand rested on the gun at her hip.

"Will you come quietly?" she asked, glancing around at the crowd of Muhajirs.

I don't know if she honestly expected me to call the people of New Medina to defend me. The idea that I would try to play Lawrence of Arabia struck me as funny as the charge that I had masterminded a revolution while running for my life through a sand storm. But Alima was another matter. While I might not be able to urge the farmers around me to defy the MACs, Alima could. And from the angry expression on her face, I thought she just might try it. I decided I had better calm things down fast.

"Of course," I said, "I will come with you," then looking at Alima, "No need to let things get out of hand."

"But this is crazy," said Alima moving toward me, "You didn't do anything. The Vegas was trying to kill us," she swung around to glare at the MAC officer, "They killed my uncle! Why don't you investigate that?"

The officer looked at Alima.

"What are you talking about?" she asked motioning the other officers to take hold of me.

"In the desert," said Alima, "We were attacked by two drones. They killed my uncle. They murdered him."

Alima's words brought the Muhajirs alive. There was a murmur of raised voices. They had already heard about Kamil's death. Some of the men and women began shouting at the MACs. One of the older men standing next to the officer spoke up.

"We want justice," he said to the officer, "We want the body of our brother Kamil found and returned. We want his murderers punished."

Now there were many more voices crying their assent. The MACs looked around nervously. There weren't enough of them if things got out of control. Their officer kept her composure. She held up her hands for silence.

"Can you show us where this happened?" she said to Alima.

"Yes," Alima said in a defiant voice, "I can take you there. The Vegas murdered my uncle."

"Very well," said the officer, speaking in a voice that could be heard around the circle of men and women gathered before the mosque, "We will recover the remains of the victim and investigate the cause of death. If there was a crime committed, we will bring the perpetrators to justice."

Quickly she ordered three of the MACs to go with Alima and begin the journey back to the crime scene. The other MACs came forward to take me into custody and transport me to Burroughs Base. The crowd had broken up into clusters of excited conversation. The two older Muhajirs were talking with the MAC commander. I had only a moment with Alima before I was hauled away.

"Will you be alright?"

"I will be fine," she said, "I only wish I could go with you."

"I wish we could be together too."

In the second after I spoke I realized how those words carried a different meaning. Alima looked up at me. Her face was powered by the dust of the Martian desert. Her eyes were framed by lines of exhaustion. Her lips were cracked from the wind. Then, without a word, she leaned up and kissed me.

The MACs jerked my arms, pulling me toward their truck.

"Don't worry," Alima called after me, "God will give us justice."

"I know," I called back, "Just please be careful out there."

"I will..." and she shouted something else but I couldn't hear it.

They pulled me away toward the truck through noise and confusion. Several of the Muhajirs were preparing to go with Alima and the MAC commander in search of uncle Kamil's body. Camels were grunting. Truck engines were revving up. Orders were being shouted.

I was hustled into the back of a truck. The MACs closed the door and started the drive out of New Medina. The last I saw of Alima she was waving to me through the dust. Yusef was by her side. As I watched her disappear into the red dust I felt as if I were falling into a dream. The orchards slipped past the windows, carried away by windmills, sailing into the distance. Martian canals floated New Medina into a hidden canyon. The black tents of the Muhajirs drifted on the wind. It was all a dream. A dream come and gone too quickly. Events moving as fast as a sand storm. The only reality a single thought: she had kissed me.

I have been in jail cells before. Like hotels, they can be given a rating for their amenities, or the lack thereof. The Burroughs Base jail got four stars.

The cells were relatively clean. The open toilet was not a source of mutating bacterial organisms. The food was edible. The guards seemed sullen but not pathological. Even my roommate was unlikely to smother me with a pillow as I slept, although as I was soon to discover, he might bore me to death. Compared to the correctional facilities in Pilgrim's Playground, the jails of Mars seemed almost comfortable.

I had slept for most of the bouncing journey back to the city. I was so exhausted by three days in the desert that I passed out. The heavy duty MAC van had brought us cross country to Burroughs Base without incident. No more sandstorms. It had deposited me at the local jail where I had been holopixed, eye-scanned, stripped, hosed down, and outfitted with yellow overalls that proudly announced I was a PRISONER in black stenciling.

I was told that I would appear before the Magistrate in two days. A public notice would be posted concerning my arrest. If no attorney (and there weren't many on Mars) came forward to represent me, I would have to represent myself. My trail date would be set by the Magistrate. I would be charged, along with Ima Maria and seven of her parishioners, with inciting a riot, destruction of public property, resisting arrest, and disturbing the social order. The minimum sentence would be five years hard labor. The maximum would be death.

As for my co-defendants, they were locked up in St. Vlad but would be transported to the city in time for our joint hearing before the Magistrate. Until then we could have no contact. In fact, I could have no contact with anyone since I was technically an undesirable until I was proven innocent. Such is the standard for Imperial Law.

I lay on the upper bunk while my roommate sat on the bed beneath me. His name was Vasili. He was a sewage treatment worker who had a problem staying sober. That much I learned in my first few minutes. The rest of Vasili's story rolled out in a long saga worthy of Tolstoy. Vasili kept reciting it in his heavily accented Russian whether I was listening or not.

"Then after I got out of trade school I worked in a laundry," I heard him say as I stared at the ceiling. After that his voice droned into white noise, masking the occasional clank and clatter of the jail around us.

I wondered where Alima was. I imagined her bouncing over the desert in another MAC van, retracing our steps to the overhang by the mesa where we had buried her uncle. I pictured her crying again as the MAC officer had the body removed. They would examine the crime scene. They would see the dead camel and the burn marks on the rocks. The remnants of our equipment would be scattered in pieces over the desert floor.

"Then my cousin Alexi got me a job with the bus line," said Vasili, "That job sucked so I started drinking again."

I wondered where Digby was. And Dr. Wu. Ima Theresa. Abba Isidore. Did they know what had happened? Were they even aware I was in jail?

Only a few days had passed since I returned home from the diocesan convention to find my life unraveling, but it seemed like months. So much had happened. Did any of them know what was going on?

"My rash came back," intoned Vasili, "that was a bitch."

And what about Clare? Had she managed to calm the revolt in the church on Home World? Or was she having to fight both The Vegas and the church conservatives as they sought to punish her for my mistakes? I wondered if she had heard any of the news about what had happened over these last days. Would she still be coming to Mars, and if so, when?

"I still can't get the sewage smell out of my nose," said Vasili, "You can take a shower but it is still there."

I looked at the ceiling. It was like a bas-relief map of the Martian desert. Rusty red and cracked. I let my eyes wander over it the way I had wandered over the surface of Mars, lost and searching for something, for anything, to make sense out of my life.

"Don't ever throw up in a sand storm," Vasili cautioned me, "I did that once and it blew right back on me."

I closed my eyes. In the distance a metal door clanged shut. Someone cursed. The bed smelled like disinfectant. Vasili droned on sitting on his bunk beneath me. Outside our tiny primoglass window I could see the first stars appear like white smudges on a black blanket. Four stars. The night was giving my jail four stars.

Saint Paul was sitting in a jail cell. His robe was dyed a bright yellow. The word PRISONER stenciled on the back.

"What are you in for?" he asked me.

"Disturbing the social order," I said.

"Me too," he said.

"But I am innocent," I said quickly.

"Same here," he replied. His large brown eyes crinkled in a smile.

"They are holding me accountable for someone else's actions," I said.

"Ditto."

"I could get five years," I said.

"Oh," he said, "I think I will get off easier than that."

"Really?" I said, "What do you think you will get?"

"Life," he said quietly, "I think I will get life."

The day I appeared before the Magistrate was something of a homecoming for me. Two MAC guards led me out of my cell.

"Check your zipper," Vasili had said in parting, "My fly was down during my last arraignment."

I was taken to a side room at the courthouse next to the jail. Ima Maria and seven of her steelworker parishioners were already there.

"We thought they had killed you," she said, "The bastards."

"They tried," I said, "but I survived. What happened, anyway? I have been out of touch and no one has told me anything."

Ima Maria began a fast run down of the past several days. After my disappearance from Burroughs Base, rumors began to fly that The Vegas had taken me for a ride into the desert. Dr. Wu and Digby were both out of sight. Abba Ambrose had pleaded ignorance, but intimated that he wasn't surprised. The Russians were silent. Abba Isidore and his community had written to the Mars Central Authority demanding an investigation, but there was no official response. The negotiations with The Vegas were still stalled. Ima Theresa had braved the sand storm to drive out to look for me, but had come up empty.

I was silent for a moment after hearing all of this recent history.

"I am really sorry to have gotten you mixed up in all of this," she said, "I don't know what else to say."

"That's funny," I said, "I have been saying the same thing to someone else for days."

"We didn't intend to start a riot," she said quietly, "We just wanted the government to take your petition seriously."

I winced. My petition. It was a reminder of how I was responsible for what had happened. I deserved to be taking the rap for this, not her.

"Let's hope the Magistrate sees it that way," I said, "A felony charge for social unrest is hard to beat ."

"Don't worry," said Ima Maria, "we will have a good defense."

I looked at her.

"Do we have a lawyer?" I asked.

"No, not exactly," she said.

I looked at the faces of her parishoners. They were smiling. Confident in their priest, in spite of it all.

"So who is going to defend us?" I asked, but the expression on Maria's face gave me the answer even before she spoke.

"Me," she said proudly.

Before I could speak a court bailiff opened the door.

"Alright," he said in Russian, "Let's go."

We shuffled into the courtroom. I checked my zipper just before the bailiff closed the door.

Chapter Eleven

Dr. Wu was sitting like the Buddha surrounded by his disciples. He was perched on a stool in his living room. Gathered around him, in chairs and on the floor, were the seven steelworkers, Ima Maria, Ima Theresa and Beth, Abba Isidore and Kalisha, Billy Wu and me. We were staring glumly into mugs of green Martian tea. We were not happy disciples. We had gathered for a strategy session following the hearing before the Magistrate. It had not gone well. He had not only refused to throw out the charges against Ima Maria and me, he had added one more. Contempt of court.

"I shouldn't have called him that name," said Maria.

"That was an unfortunate choice," said Dr. Wu.

"At least some of you were released," said Kalisha quietly. Isidore squeezed her hand and nodded.

"That is something to be grateful for," agreed Dr. Wu.

The steelworkers had been charged only as accessories, fined and put on probation. Ima Maria and I were left to face the felony charges with the full five years at hard labor as the penalty if found guilty. Or worse.

"We're going to need a proper lawyer," said Ima Theresa, "Somebody who doesn't climb on chairs." She shot a look at Ima Maria. "No offense, Maria."

"No, it's true," Maria said with her head bowed, "I really screwed up."

The steelworkers nearest to her reached out to pat her back in reassurance.

"Don't blame yourself," I said, "They weren't going to let us off anyway. We were lucky to just be bailed out until the trial." I looked up at Dr. Wu. "Thank you for doing that, Dr. Wu," I said.

He gave me a smile and waved his small hands.

"Who knows a lawyer?" asked Ima Theresa, "That's the question."

"We have a lawyer in our congregation," said Abba Isidore, "He helped us make our appeal to the Mars Central Authority, but he is too scared to do any more."

"Intimidation," muttered Ima Maria.

"Sadly, that is the case," said Dr. Wu, "The Vegas wants no more interference while they are negotiating with the government."

"They proved that out in the desert," I said, "They were willing to get rid of me permanently. In the end, they just killed an innocent man."

"Maybe you better go back into hiding," said Theresa.

"I don't believe that will be necessary now," said Dr. Wu, "The Vegas will let the law do the work for them. If they can get the bishop out of the way legally, they will have no need to risk any further extreme measures on their own."

Ima Maria started to cry.

"I am so sorry," she kept saying. I went over to comfort her. It seemed so out of character for her to show such vulnerability. It was as if she embodied all of our feelings of weakness before the power of The Vegas.

The meeting sort of dissolved after that. We all agreed to regroup before the trial. Dr. Wu said he would work with me on a strategy for our defense. He suggested that Maria get some rest. The steelworkers filed out, supporting her in a circle of broad shoulders and strong arms. Isidore and Kalisha looked like angels with broken wings as they said their good-byes, promising to talk to their lawyer friend one last time, but not holding out much hope. I stayed behind with Billy Wu, Beth and Theresa.

"Ok," Ima Theresa said, when the others had gone, "What are our options?"

"We don't have any options," I said, "unless you count a miracle as an option."

Dr. Wu laughed quietly.

"I would have thought a miracle would be something you expected."

"They happen all the time on Mars," said Beth.

Theresa ran a hand through the bristles of her white hair.

"Miracles happen," she said, "but making them happen is a little out of our league."

"Perhaps," said Dr. Wu, "but there may be a way to invite one to happen."

Beth and I both spoke at once, "How?"

Dr. Wu leaned toward us.

"By giving the miracle a name," he said.

He paused, adjusting his small body to balance on the edge of his chair.

"I was sitting in my garden last night, listening to my plants," he said, "And they spoke to me."

"Wonderful," said Beth.

"Cool," said Billy.

Ima Theresa looked at me to see if I understood what had just been said. I looked back and shrugged.

"Ok, I give up," Ima Theresa said, "I don't speak plant, so please tell me what is the name of the miracle that can get us out of this mess?"

Dr. Wu leaned forward to whisper the name to us as though he were speaking an incantation to conjure up unseen hope.

"Digby," he said with a sly smile, "The miracle is named Digby."

"Excellent," said Beth quietly.

"Digby?" I asked, "Why Digby? He isn't even here. We haven't seen him for days."

Dr. Wu nodded happily, "Which is why I came to see that he must be the essential ingredient to the process."

"I'm sorry," said Ima Theresa standing up in exasperation, "but I don't get it."

"Another reason to find him," said Dr. Wu. He rubbed his small hands together as if he were thoroughly pleased with the way things were going.

"Billy?" I said "You want to jump in here?"

Billy hunched his handsome shoulders.

"I told you my uncle was a mystical guy. All I can tell you is that his intuitions are never wrong."

"Find Digby," I said, "That's the answer?"

"Trust my plants," said Dr. Wu, "They are very wise."

And with that said, he proceeded to give us our marching orders on the road to a miracle.

The next day we put Dr. Wu's strategy into operation. He was going to make discreet enquiries into the negotiations going on behind the scenes between The Vegas and the government. The Vegas lawyers were coming back into town and Dr. Wu was going to find out all that he could about their plans to seal the deal for the Mega Mars project. He would work quietly through his contacts with Metropolitan Seraphim and the Mars bankers.

Ima Theresa and Billy Wu were going to be in touch with Alima. They were going to follow up on the results of the investigation by the MACs into the murder of uncle Kamil to see if any connection could be made to The Vegas. I wanted that job, but was over ruled by Dr. Wu because I might not be someone the MACs would talk to. I think he also suspected that I would get too emotionally involved. Good call.

Ima Maria was to stay camped out with Isidore and Kalisha at my place. Their job was to keep her out of trouble. They had also kindly volunteered to clean it up for me.

As for me, I was to find Digby. He had done another of his periodic disappearing acts and his ComCom was only taking messages.

But what could Digby do?

"I don't know," said Dr. Wu when I asked him, "I was contemplating the Tao while sitting in my rooftop garden. Like the Tao, Digby is everywhere, but he is nowhere. He is both seen and unseen. Like the ten thousand things, he is a mystery. Therefore, he must be essential."

"But how do I find out where he is if he is nowhere? Or how do I nail someone down who seems to be in all places at the same time? Does the Tao give me any clues on that?"

"I've thought about that too," said Dr. Wu, "I think my meditations have given me an answer. Negative space. Over these last few days the only person not in the picture has been Digby. He has been missing. Absent. My plants helped me to understand that this is why he is so crucial. Because he is in negative space."

"Negative space?"

Dr. Wu nodded, "Yes, exactly."

I rubbed my head, "I'm sorry but I still don't get this."

Dr. Wu pushed his glasses up his small nose and looked at me intently.

"It is a basic philosophy behind Chinese art. When you look at a painting, the spaces between the objects are as important as the objects themselves. They are negative space. They hold everything together. Therefore, they are critical to the whole work. Without them, nothing would make sense. In my meditation with the plants I began to focus not on what we could see, but on what was missing. What was between the lines, so to speak."

"Digby?"

Dr. Wu slowly nodded, "Digby is negative space. Therefore, he must be the most important factor in the equation. We must find him. Then the picture will begin to make sense."

"So my job is to go out into negative space?"

"Exactly," he said, "Go to where you think Digby will not be."

"Find Digby by going to where he is not?"

Dr. Wu laughed and clapped his hands, his head nodding vigorously.

"Negative space?" I asked again.

"Negative space," he smiled.

With nothing more to go on than Dr. Wu's intuition gathered from the Tao, Chinese art and a garden full of deep thinking petunias, I began my quest. As far as I could tell, there was a lot of negative space to cover.

Mars is as big as Earth. If you compare the landmass of Earth above the oceans to the landmass of Mars, they are almost exactly the same. That's a lot of landmass.

Out there, somewhere I least expected to find him, was Digby. Why I needed to find him and how was not clear. In fact, it was the opposite of clear. It was opaque. Still, everyone else was doing something. I did not want to just sit in my house and wait for the axe to fall. Even if the search for Digby proved to be a waste of time, it would keep my mind off impending disaster. So I trusted Dr. Wu's instincts. Maybe finding Digby would be the miracle we needed after all. I had tried calling Digby, of course, but only got his usual message, "gone prospecting." If he was out in the desert, he might not even be able to respond for days.

But would he be in the desert?

That was another question. It didn't seem to make sense for Digby to be wandering around in Dragon Month. He was too experienced to risk being out in the open during sand storm season. No, for Digby, the desert was not negative space. It was his natural habitat. If I was going to go where I would be least likely to find him I had to be counter intuitive. Although it was the longest long shot I could imagine, I decided to start my quest for Digby in the one place on Mars as contrary to desert as I could find.

I drove to New Shanghai. I borrowed Dr. Wu's ATV and just did it. Of all the places Digby might go, the least likely would be the perfect burbs. Digby was the antithesis of the neat and manicured Martian. He was old school. A prospector. A loner. A man outside the conventions of society. If New Shanghai was as conventional as it got on Mars, it could be the gateway to the negative space where I might find him. At least, that was what my own instincts told me.

Abba Isidore and Kalisha had called ahead. By the time I reached New Shanghai it was evening. They had arranged for me to stay in their house. I was greeted by a pleasant middle aged woman who was in charge of things while they were away. She had prepared some dinner for me. As I sat in their polished kitchen I ask if she knew Digby.

"Everyone knows Digby," she had replied.

"But have you seen him recently?"

"No," she had told me, "he never comes to New Shanghai. I've only seen him at charity events. He is such an odd little man."

"Would there be any events in town that he might attend?"

"Not during Dragon Month," she said, "You can never get a good turnout in Dragon Month. Weather is too unpredictable."

"Does he have any relatives or friends in New Shanghai?"

"As far as I know, he doesn't have any family," she told me, "He just seems to pop up and disappear."

I thanked her for the dinner. She left me with the wish that I find Digby. "He is such a strange little man," were her parting words.

The next morning I sat in the neat kitchen, drinking expensive coffee and trying to let my mind search for the unexpected. If New Shanghai was negative space, maybe it wasn't quite negative enough. What was even more incongruous for Digby? I finished the coffee and went to take a bath, like the fresh brewed coffee, another luxury to indulge.

In the bathroom I found my answer.

They say that Martin Luther had his inspiration for the Protestant Reformation while sitting on the toilet in his monastery one cold morning. I had mine laying in a whirlpool bath. I had been seduced by the sheer luxury of it. Back in Burroughs Base I had to make do with a regular visit to the public baths. But in this suburban home I had encountered a state-of-the-art Martian bathroom, complete with a bathtub that not only heated the water but swirled it around to massage tired muscles. I had climbed in, switched it on, and sighed as the jets of bubbling water caressed my body.

Suddenly, I had my Archimedes moment. My eyes popped open and I almost quoted the ancient Greek with a shout of Eureka. If New Shanghai was the last place to find a guy like Digby, then the last place in New Shanghai to look would be the most perfect and pampered space it had to offer. The Sans Souci. The most exclusive spa on Mars.

I almost jumped out of the tub with the excitement of my discovery. Almost. But I figured a few more minutes in the bubbles wouldn't make that much difference.

The Sans Souci was not the product of any great detective work on my part. It was more of a subliminal discovery. I had the name and the image imprinted in my brain by the holopix billboards that were projected all along the highway coming into New Shanghai. A rather strange, and you might even say slightly disturbing, variation on the little green man advertisement had come into my mind while I lay in the bathtub.

The image was of a curvaceous little green woman floating in a whirlpool bath with a towel wrapped around her head. Two small antennae poked out through the towel as she looked down on the passing motorists with a seductive smile. PAMPER YOUR INNER MARTIAN the sign had said. The Sans Souci, the ultimate spa for those who can afford the very best.

I checked the ComCom for details. The Sans Souci was an exclusive spa and resort that offered the full range of comforts for those who could indulge themselves. Martian mud baths. Martian hot rock massage. Martian makeovers. It was a private hideaway where the Martian elite could go to lose themselves for a week of private preening.

"You can't get much more negative than that," I said looking at the ComCom. I dialed up for directions. The face of a young Chinese woman appeared before me. She had the sculpted looks of expensive enhancements. Her eyes stared back at me with the lazy self-assurance that she was already beautiful and I was just a wannabe.

"Can you tell me if you have a guest staying there by the name of Digby?" I asked, but she only stared back at me with all the warmth of a mannequin.

"I am sorry," she said in perfect Mandarin, "but we do not give out the names of our guests. Would you care to make a reservation?"

I knew her hand was on the cut off button so I spoke quickly.

"Ah, yes, I would," I said.

She paused.

"And when would that be?" she asked in a bored tone.

"Hmmm," I stalled, "Do you take walk-ins?"

She looked at me as if I had said lepers.

"Just a moment," she said. I thought she might cut me off, but maybe after my own bubble bath, I looked just good enough to pass.

"We do have a day's reservation available now," she said, "but you would need to arrive by 10:00am".

"Great," I said, "I can make that."

"The name," she asked.

"Lucky," I said, "Bishop Lucky."

"We will see you at 10:00 am," she said and disappeared.

I grabbed my bags and ran for the ATV. Either I had just had a wild hunch that would pay off, or, I was about to get my negative spaces waxed.

I was trying to walk on my heels. The foam spacers between my toes kept slipping. The pedicurist had told me to let the polish dry for at least fifteen minutes before I removed them, but once she left me in the chair alone I decided it was time to search for Digby. I hobbled out of the room and duck walked down the hall.

The San Souci is an elegant spa. It sits up in the hills above New Shanghai. A private drive leads to an ornate wrought iron gate with the double "S" initials of Sans Souci curling around the bars. A man in a tailored pair of pink overalls greeted me, checked my name on a list and let me drive in.

I drove past neatly trimmed lawns, a rarity on Mars. They were the clear signs of conspicuous consumption, an announcement that this establishment had water to waste. They were overflowing with more plants than even Dr. Wu could imagine. The entrance itself was an elaborate portico of polished Martian red stone columns. An attendant welcomed me to the Sans Souci, gave me a ticket for my ATV and drove it away.

Once inside, a twin sister of the woman who had answered my call processed me into the spa. Soft Russian folk music was playing. The air smelled like lavender. She led me to a changing room where I stripped off my clothes and put on a pink bathrobe and slippers, both tastefully monogrammed with the double "S" in gold. I had checked what I desired off a menu, beginning with the pedicure I thought would be the least confining choice as I began my search for Digby. In keeping with the fashion on Home World I had chosen to have my nails done in blue, the color worn by men.

I passed a few other guests as I padded down the polished hallway. I peeked into rooms where other men and women were lying face down on tables with hot stones on their backs. But no Digby. I went on to the mud baths and found disembodied heads poking out of pools of red clay, each turbaned with pink towels, but still no Digby. I even hopped out to the pool area where a few patrons were sipping Martian Mai Tais in the shade of multi-colored canopies, but Digby was not among them. I got some curious looks, but such is the privacy policy of the Sans Souci that no one stopped me on my ambles through the resort.

I had just about given up when I heard a familiar voice speak my name.

"Bishop?" it said.

I turned, and there, standing in a crisp pink tunic and white shorts, wearing an enormous wide brimmed straw hat, holding a cigar, was Digby. He looked me up and down, stopping to admire my bright blue toes.

"Bishop?" he said again, "What are you doing here?"

"Digby?" I stammered, "I was looking for you."

Digby shushed me with one finger to his lips, looking around quickly.

"Please," he stage whispered, "Don't call me that." He slipped his arm through mine and swept me off down a side hallway. "Around here I am known as Almos. Count Almos Gazda."

"Count what…?"

"It's a long story. Just don't call me Digby."

We made our way down a covered walkway with a view of the Sans Souci gardens.

"Well, I'll be," he said laughing, "I never expected to see you turn up here. I thought I had the perfect hideout."

"You either," I said, "Or, I mean, you too. Or, well, what I mean is, I did expect to find you here, even if I didn't. Which is why I did."

Digby gave me a quizzical look.

"You've been in the steam bath too long," he said, "You're not making sense."

"Never mind," I said quickly, "It's just something Dr. Wu told me. Look, I need to talk to you."

"Sure," said Digby, "let's go to my office."

"Your office?" I asked, duck-walking along as quickly as I could next to him.

"That's right," said Digby, and gesturing with an expansive wave of his hand, he laughed, "I own this place."

Digby's office had a glass wall that gave a panoramic view of the mountains that surrounded Sans Souci like a barrier against reality. We sat in soft body shaped chairs. The walls were tastefully decorated with paintings by one of Mars's most celebrated artists, although I am embarrassed to admit that I can't recall the name. Along one wall, behind a huge ornate desk, obviously a Chinese antique imported from Earth, was a built in book case with a number of rock and crystal specimens. As he handed me a snifter of brandy, Digby noticed me looking at them.

"Mementoes of my first discoveries," he said, looking at the rock collection, "They are the basis of my fortune."

Digby settled himself into a chair opposite me. He had tossed his straw hat aside. He leaned back, stretching his short legs before him. I noticed his toenails were also polished blue as they peeped out of expensive sandals. He took a sip of brandy and smiled at me.

"I guess you are surprised, huh?" he said.

"I am dumbfounded," I said.

Digby laughed.

"I suppose most people would be. They only see me as Digby, the prospector."

He gazed out the glass wall toward the layer caked mountains rising above New Shanghai. "That is me," he said quietly, "I will always be a prospector. Out looking for what I lost." Then turning back to me he swept one arm in a great arc to take in everything around us, "But now this is me too. I just prefer to keep the two worlds apart. That's why, when I come here, I turn off the Digby part of me. I am sorry that it made me hard to find."

"But how did you come by all of this?" I asked taking a sniff at my brandy. It smelled expensive.

"I listened," he said simply.

Digby, or Count Gazda, settled himself into his chair and told me his story.

"When I was a young man I met Zhaohui, the scientist who would come to be known as Dr. Wu. He was just beginning his work terraforming Mars. I was a day laborer then, working for his company when it was just getting started. Those were great days. Neither one of us had anything, but we both dreamed big. I told him that I wanted to be a prospector. I wanted to have my own mine and never be poor again. He told me to do what he did, follow the way of the Tao. Just go out into the desert and listen to the rocks. It sounded crazy, but hey, in those days, I was crazy. So I tried it. I roamed around the desert listening to the rocks. One day I heard my instincts tell me to start digging. So I dug. And the Tao was right. I dug up a fortune."

"You are rich?" I asked the rhetorical question.

Digby nodded.

"Afraid so," he said, "I control 80% of the precious minerals on Mars and Mars is the mother lode."

He smiled in an almost shy way.

I looked over at the rock collection. Uranium. Gold. Silver. And God knew what else.

"And no one knows you own all this?"

"Oh, a handful of people do," said Digby, "The Co-Governors and the head of the Mars Bank. They know me as Count Gazda, the wealthy

Hungarian who owns most of what is under the surface of Mars. The rest of the world knows me as Digby. So I can come and go as I please. Sort of invisible. I like it that way."

In the Bible it says that scales fell from the eyes of Saint Paul when he had his revelation. If I had any scales on my eyes, they had just dropped into my brandy.

"You are the one behind the hold up in the Mega Mars project," I breathed.

Digby gave me a grin and lifted his brandy snifter to toast my deduction.

"It was the least I could do," he said, "I let them know quietly that I had grave concerns about it. I hinted I might even need to transfer my funds to Home World. Those dollars are behind the whole colonization economy of Mars, so they had to listen."

"So you've stopped the project," I said sitting up in my chair with a broad smile, but Digby held up one hand to stop me.

"No," he said firmly, "I have slowed it down, but I have not stopped it. The Vegas have as much money as I do. They also have their claws in a lot of politicians and a lot of finance people. They have muscle and they aren't afraid to use it. Right now we are at a standoff. But unless something breaks our way I am not certain if I can hold them off forever."

"They tried to kill me," I said quietly.

Digby drew in a sudden gulp of air.

"I had no idea," he said suddenly, "are you alright?"

I nodded, "I am now, but it was a close call. I tried to get out of town but they chased me down in the desert and almost turned me to toast. I think they will try to hit anyone who gets in their way."

Digby sat his glass down and stood up.

"That's why I took off," he said, "After putting the squeeze on the government I thought it was better to hide out for a while. I'm sorry I wasn't there to help you."

"That's ok," I said, "You did enough just putting the brakes on the Mega Mars deal."

"Do you need to hide here? I can put you in a sauna where they will never find you."

I shook my head.

"Not necessary," I said, "Ima Maria has taken care of that."

Digby gave me a what-are-we-talking-about look.

"You better sit back down and let me catch you up on what's been happening," I said. Digby poured us both some more brandy and I told him the story up to the point where I got my toes polished.

John the Baptist was bent over with his ear against the desert floor. He was wearing sunglasses and a pink robe.

"What are you doing?" I asked him.

"Listening," he said.

"Do you hear anything?"

"Just the Tao," he said.

"What's it say?"

"You can't judge a book by its cover."

"What does that mean?"

"Do you see that little man coming this way?"

"Yes."

"Well he's not what he appears to be."

"He looks like a normal guy..."

"Exactly," said John the Baptist, "Negative space."

The next morning I was sitting in Digby's office again, drinking orange juice and eating a cheese omelette. He was wearing imported silk pajamas from China and smoking a cigar.

I had called Dr. Wu on the ComCom when I woke up. He told me that The Vegas lawyers were trying to rig the verdict of the impending trial. He said that there was no word from Ima Theresa because the sand storms were causing bad reception. Ima Maria was behaving herself, but Abba Isidore had come up empty on finding a lawyer. As for his own investigations, he said that his sources expected the government to give in to The Vegas, even though they were under some tremendous pressure not to. After this run down he asked me about my progress. I told him I had found Digby, but could not tell him where.

"Of course you cannot tell me," he said, "because it is in negative space. But is he the miracle we need?"

"I'm not sure," I told him, "He seems miraculous, but I don't know what else he can do to help."

Dr. Wu had been quiet for a moment. His small face looked like a disappointed Buddha frowning at me on the ComCom screen.

"I am sorry to hear that," he said slowly, "I had thought Digby was the answer."

"But why, Dr. Wu?" I asked, "Why would Digby be the answer?"

"I have no idea at all," he said looking at me, as puzzled as I was, "It just came to me while I was listening to my plants. Perhaps I should have listened harder."

I started to say that Digby had told me he followed Dr. Wu's advice to listen to rocks and found a fortune, but I thought that might break confidence with Digby so instead I just babbled, "Well, maybe we've come to a dead end."

Dr. Wu stopped frowning and looked at me, "Say that again, please."

I paused for a second and then repeated, "I said, maybe we have come to a dead end."

"Excellent deduction!" he cried.

"I'm sorry…"

"A dead end. Exactly. We are at the end. We must go to the beginning!"

"I still don't get it…" I stammered.

"That is not important," said Dr. Wu smiling, "The Tao doesn't care. Just tell Digby to go to the beginning. Tell him to go there and listen. That's where the miracle will happen. I am sure of it. You must tell Digby to go to the beginning. Do it right away."

That is why, as I was finishing my omelette, I told Digby what Dr. Wu had said.

"But I am not sure what it means," I said, patting my mouth with a napkin.

"Zhaohui is never wrong," said Digby, "It has to mean something."

"I wish I could stay and try to find out," I said, "but I have to get back to town for the trial. I can't risk being caught out here in a sand storm and miss it. Then they would really throw the book at me. Do you want to come back with me?"

Digby seemed lost in thought.

"No," he said slowly, "not now. I better think about this and see if I can come up with anything. You go ahead. I'll be there later, don't worry." I left him standing before the windows of his office, looking out onto the expanse of Mars.

I drove between the wrought iron gates and through the tidy streets of New Shanghai. The street sweepers were out in force to keep Dragon Month from ruining the neat appearance of the neighborhoods. The mall parking lot was crowded. I drove onto the highway leading back to Burroughs Base. The Martian desert was a quiet landscape of reddish orange. The sun watched over it through the pink air. A gentle breeze pushed past me as I drove.

God is in heaven and all is right on Mars, I thought. All, but my life. I was about to stand trial with little hope of getting anything less than five years hard labor. If that meant five years of breaking rocks, there were a lot of rocks on Mars to break. The government was about to cave in to The Vegas, so everything I had been through, and put other people through, would be for nothing. Uncle Kamil was dead and unless the MACSs and Ima Theresa had turned up a smoking gun there was little hope that The Vegas could be tied to the crime.

"What else could go wrong?" I said out loud.

That's when the ComCom rang.

Chapter Twelve

"Archbishop Clare is coming to Mars."

Abba Ambrose's face wobbled on the holopix as I bounced down the highway toward Burroughs Base. His narrow set eyes peered down the slope of his great aquiline nose to a point just between my eyes. I could tell he was enjoying letting me have it in that exact spot.

"She has been informed of the felony charges brought against you by the state. She left Home World on a First Class express flight. She will be attending the trial. In the likely event of your conviction she will need to appoint a new bishop for the Diocese of Mars."

"Any more good news to share?" I asked Abba Ambrose.

He scowled back at me.

"No, that is all," he said, "I knew that you would want to be informed."

"That's very gracious of you," I said, "as always."

He hung up after a perfunctory farewell, leaving me to contemplate the arrival of Ima Clare into the expanding soap opera of my life. I wasn't really surprised that she was coming. I was certain that she would have heard about my felony indictment. I couldn't communicate with her directly while under suspension, but Abba Ambrose could and I was sure that he wasted no time getting all of the gory details to her. It would greatly weaken her position while strengthening his.

I wondered what impact my arrest and trial would have on the church on Home World. If I were convicted it would make Clare's judgment appear flawed. With the pressure of The Vegas eating away at the foundations of her support, it could even force her out of office. Or split the church. Either way the outcome would be a disaster.

Now she was coming to Mars to look into the face of the guy who made it all possible. I looked off the road to see if there were any convenient sand traps I could drive into.

I made it back to Burroughs Base just as another sand storm hit. Thank God for small blessings, I thought as I shucked off my overalls in the dust room of my house.

Ima Maria was waiting for me. She was slumped in a chair watching the news on the ComCom. I noticed that they had put the place back together. Even Rasputin had returned.

"Have you heard?" she asked me as I walked in.

"About Clare?" I asked.

She nodded. I nodded. We both sighed.

"Where are Isidore and Kalisha?" I asked.

"Over at the church," said Ima Maria, "They went to assassinate Ambrose."

I laughed. "Anything on the news?" I asked her. She switched it off.

"I was looking to see if there was any word about the murder investigation," she said leaning back on my old sofa. "There was a mention of it. A death under suspicious circumstances they called it. Still under investigation. But no more information than that."

I closed my eyes and thought about Alima. Did Ima Theresa find her? Had they returned Kamil's body to New Medina? Did the MACs find anything to link the Vegas to the murder? So many questions with no answers until Theresa could get back. I listened to the pelting of sand against the windows. If she could get back. She might be stuck out at New Medina for days. Even weeks.

"Tony." I opened my eyes. Ima Maria was looking at me. She had never called me Tony before.

"I really am so sorry," she said.

I looked at her. There was a strange serenity to her expression. Her face, usually so expressive and animated, was like a pool of water undisturbed by any tremor, deep and constant.

"Listen," she said, "I want to tell you something. It's not an excuse. It's just an explanation. I think I owe you that."

The dusty light from the window bathed one half of her face in a soft orange glow.

"I know you may think I am just short tempered and crazy," she said, and when I started to speak she held up her hand, "No need to try to say otherwise. I messed this up because I get emotional. I know that. And it's true. I can get..." she searched for the word, "...angry. But there is a reason."

I shifted my weight to sit facing her on the sofa. Only the wind driving sand against the house made any sound in the space between us.

"When I was a young woman" she said softly, "I married a Native guy from Machu Picchu. Do you know it?"

I nodded. Machu Picchu was The Vegas outlet in the Andes, their second largest operation in the southern part of West Hem. It was built around ancient Inca ruins. I had seen a ComCom ad once that showed tourists playing roulette where the Incas once worshipped the Sun.

"He turned out to be part the *Cheistas*. Do you know who they are?"

"Revolutionaries," I said, "Outlaws. They tried to blow up the casino at Amazon Adventure."

"That's right," she said, "Outlaws against the outlaws. He was... we were... part of that. When he got arrested they tortured him before he died. There was nothing I could do. When I saw what they did to him, I broke down. I fell apart. I ran. I got scared and I ran. I deserted everything he believed in...everything...and I just...ran away."

She took a deep breath and looked at me.

"That's all I want to say. I'm not looking for sympathy. My story is no big deal. A lot of people in the church have hard luck stories. Probably you too. But I wanted you to know why I act the way I do. Why I can get so angry. I think it's how I cover up the fear. I guess I have never stopped running. I'm sorry."

She sat still, looking down, her hands clasped tightly. I reached over and placed my hand on her's.

"Maria, you don't ever have to apologize for having survived."

She looked at me.

"I didn't live what you have lived," I said, "but I understand enough to know that anger is what has kept many of us alive when we had nothing else to keep us going."

Ima Maria nodded. "I just wanted you to know who I was. Who I am."

The wind rattled the windows.

"It's ok," I said, "we'll get through this. Not just because we are survivors. But because we are friends."

I think Maria was going to say something, but just then Isidore and Kalisha returned, flooding the room with their cheerful voices. Maria and I exchanged a last look, but for people like us, that was enough.

Jesus was in a garden. He was praying.

"I am sorry I interrupted you," I said. "Would you like for me to leave?"

"I'm afraid you have to," he said, "I'm afraid they all have to."

"But how about you? Don't you want to leave? It's getting late."

"Oh yes," he said, "I want to leave. Believe me. But I am going to stay."

"Why?"

"Because, like you say, it is getting late."

That night Dr. Wu came over for what felt like a last supper. Kalisha had made mushroom soup. We sat around my living room talking. Ima Maria said very little and ate even less. Abba Isidore tried to find something hopeful in a report he had seen on the ComCom: the MACs had returned from the desert with pieces of the mining drone they had found. It was another thirty second item on the news, but there was no mention of any concrete results from the investigation.

Dr. Wu said that he had gotten a brief message from Digby.

"He is going to the beginning," Dr. Wu had said when I asked him what was in the message.

"What does that mean?"

"I have no idea," he laughed, "but I am sure it is good news."

Isidore and Kalisha agreed, but I knew they were in the silver lining business. I felt claustrophobic sitting in my house so I decided to go and do the only thing left to do. I was going to church to pray.

"Be careful," Kalisha had said, "The sand storm is still blowing."

I promised I would. For a moment I thought Ima Maria might join me, but she seemed so tired that she decided to turn in early. Abba Isidore wanted to watch the news in case there was any more information coming out about the murder investigation. Kalisha was talking to Dr. Wu, so I slipped out to go to St. Michael and All Angels.

I decided to walk. The sand was whipping around, but nothing like what I had experienced with Alima in the desert. I had my goggles on and my face covered. The street lights glowed dimly through the orange sand-fog. Few ATVs were out on the streets. I bent my head and walked toward the church.

When I arrived it was empty but the lights were on. Unlike church buildings on Home World, Martian places of worship keep their doors unlocked. Theft is not a major problem on Mars because there are few places to run to with stolen goods. Besides, there were no valuables in the church. Martian crosses are made of steel, not gold.

I went through the silent church to the statue of Mary that is tucked away in a side chapel. On my first visit to St. Michael and All Angels I was grateful to discover that she was not the artistic work of Mrs. Quigly, but a classic statue imported from Home World. She had the serene face I needed to see. With her head slightly inclined to watch me as I knelt, draped in a soft blue head covering that reminded me of Alima's hajib, Mary sparkled with the candlelight that flickered from the votive lights at her feet.

I prayed for her help. For Alima. For uncle Kamil. For all the friends who were now part of my life. For Clare, racing toward Mars through the cold silence of space. I prayed for the miracle we needed. Finally I lit a candle and turned to go.

Abba Ambrose was standing in the aisle, watching me.

I walked toward him, not sure what to say, but drawn to him just the same. When I came close I saw his sharp features waver in the dim light. Was it embarrassment? I thought so. It is a strange thing to see someone you don't like in the act of prayer. I know because I have been in that position before. I have seen men and women I disliked praying. It troubled me in a way that words cannot easily describe. Somehow it robbed them of the mask I had put on them. It made them more human, more real than I wanted them to be. It reminded me that, like myself, they have hearts and hopes and hurts. I wondered if Ambrose was just as troubled by being an unintentional voyeur to my devotions.

"Good evening, Abba," I said quietly.

"Good evening, Bishop," he said.

We waited for the other to speak. The empty room seemed to press us together with its silence.

"I did not mean to disturb you," he said at last.

"That's ok," I said, "I was just praying."

Outside a sudden gust of wind wailed around the roof of the

church.

"I am here for the same reason," he said and then seemed to hesitate, unsure what else to add to his simple statement.

"I hope you will remember me when you do," I said.

He looked up down his long nose like a scarecrow made sad by a flock of crows.

"I will," he said.

I gave him a weak smile and nodded slightly. I felt the same embarrassment rise in my chest. I had not remembered him when I prayed.

"I will remember you too," I stammered.

"Thank you," he said almost in a whisper and looked away.

"Well, good night," I said and turned to go.

"Good night," he said from behind me. My own footsteps were all I heard walking to the door. I knew he was still standing there, watching me leave. I wondered what he must be thinking. I wondered if he felt as unsettled as I was feeling. I wondered if Mary could hear me from across the room as I prayed his name before I left the church.

I was half way home when a late model ATV pulled up next to me on the street. In the dust whipped night, beneath the dim streetlights, it had emerged like a specter with yellow eyes. Two large figures stepped out, their faces hidden by dust masks and goggles.

"Get in," said one of them. I didn't even bother to ask where we were going.

I couldn't see anything in the sand that blurred the streets, but I knew we were back at the warehouse when we pulled in. I took a deep breath as I got out, flinching from what I knew was to come. But instead of pounding me again, the two heavies just took me by the arms and led me to an office at the back of the building. They knocked once, opened the door, and escorted me into a room cluttered with file boxes and files of holodiscs.

"Ah, Bishop," a man said, standing up from behind a metal desk, coming around to shake my hand. He was as tall as I am, with a face sculpted by enhancements. His hands were smooth. His clothes tailored in Home World fashion, a form fitting jacket over pleated trousers and soft shoes. A platinum pinky ring glistened in the artificial light. When he took my hand I could feel the strength beneath the suit.

"Thank you for coming," he said with a smile that reminded me of a piranha, pure white teeth polished like pearls. "Won't you sit down?"

He motioned me to a chair and sat on the edge of the desk. I could not see the other two men standing behind me against the wall but I didn't have to. I swallowed and tried to breathe slowly.

"Let me come right to the point," he said smiling, "I represent certain parties that would like to help you out of your present difficulties. I believe you will understand what I mean. Your trial is coming up day after tomorrow, is it not?"

"It is," I said. My voice sounded hollow. I cleared my throat.

"Exactly," he said, "day after tomorrow. I am afraid the outcome looks rather predictable."

"Oh, I don't know," I said but had no idea what that meant.

"Five years at hard labor," said the man without blinking, "And who knows what could happen to you while you were incarcerated." He frowned in mock concern. "Not to mention your co-defendant," he said slowly, "Her situation might be even more..." he paused, "... perilous."

He waited while his words hung in the air. I became conscious of a small ceiling fan slowly rotating above me. The man sighed and shook his head.

"But it doesn't have to be that way," he said at last, "There is an alternative." He stood up and walked back to his chair. He sat down and leaned across the desk, folding his hands before him as if in prayer.

I didn't want to imagine to what gods.

"The parties of whom I spoke are not without influence," he said smoothly, "With your cooperation they might be able to advocate for a suspended sentence. Not only for you, but for your co-defendant as well."

I felt a small trickle of sweat run down the back of my neck.

"What kind of cooperation?" I asked.

The man twisted his pinky ring as if giving my question some thought.

"Well," he said carefully, "a guilty plea, an admission that you were misguided in your actions, an appeal for clemency with a promise to forego any more opposition to development efforts designed only to bring financial benefit to the community...these kinds of statements could inspire the court to act with compassion." He looked at me with a lazy stare.

"You mean, plead guilty and promise to shut up," I said flatly.

He smiled, "A less than elegant turn of phrase, but not inaccurate."

"And what if I don't cooperate?" I asked. Another trickle of sweat tickled my spine.

The man did not answer. He only watched me. Seconds ticked by. The ceiling fan pushed hot air over my damp hairline.

"I will need to think about it. Talk to...my co-defendant," I said.

"Of course," he said quietly, "give it some very careful thought."

No one moved.

"Can I go?" I asked.

"My drivers will take you straight home," he said without standing, "I am sure you are anxious to get back to your friends."

I stood up on wobbly legs but tried to appear calm as I moved toward the door. Just as one of the heavies opened the door the man spoke to my back.

"Be sure to tell Maria that we are thinking of her too," he said.

I didn't turn around. I just walked out to the car and let them drive me home.

That night I sat alone with Ima Maria in Dr. Wu's roof garden. I told her what had happened. I told her what the man with the platinum ring had told me. The last of the sand storm scrapped against the dome as she listened.

"Too bad you couldn't kick him in the cajones," she said when I finished, giving me a weak smile.

"Maria," I said, "This is serious. He wasn't kidding. You know these guys. You know what they are capable of."

"I know," she said, "but I am tired of running. I say we stand our ground and give them our best shot."

We were sitting almost knee to knee on the old crates in his garden. I reached over and took her hand.

"No matter what it costs us?"

"No matter what," she said.

We sat for a moment, holding hands like two teenagers.

"You sure?" I asked.

"I'm sure," she said, "Besides, Mars is the end of the road. Where else are we going to go? This may not be much of a planet yet, but it's our planet."

She squeezed my hand once more and stood up.

"See you in the morning," she said. She walked down the spiral stairs. I watched her disappear. I sat in the garden for a while, but Dr. Wu's plants were silent under the twin moons of Mars. I blew out the candle and went to bed.

I stood by the pool of water beneath the great Roman arches of the space terminal. The origami mobile hung above me like paper swords. People hustled past me, rendering me all but invisible in the crowd. I had been standing there for thirty minutes. I was waiting for Clare.

Abba Ambrose had called unexpectedly the night before.

"As the Chair of Standing Committee," he said, "I have the privilege of meeting the Archbishop when she arrives tomorrow from Home World, but under the circumstances I thought you might want to be the one to welcome her."

"Thank you, Ambrose," I had said, "that is very kind of you." Our two ComCom images had floated before one another for only a moment before he said good-bye.

The holopix information board announced the arrival of the transit from Earth. I looked up at the glowing Chinese and Russian letters and took a deep breath. The first trickle of passengers emerged from Customs. Friends and family rushed forward to greet them, snatch bags to carry, and walk away in a chatter of conversation. I waited, craning my neck to see Clare when she came through the swinging doors. More people passed into the terminal. Finally, stepping out of the doorway, I saw the tall man I had known as a woman for all these years. She was dressed in her habit. She wore soft Chinese boots in black. Her sunflower eyes scanned the crowd until they found me. With her travel bag in hand she walked toward me.

I had rehearsed this moment. I thought I should extend my hand. I imagined my saying something neutral like "how good to see you." I would take her bag and show her the way to the ATV. But In the end, seeing her for the first time in so long, after all that had happened, I just stood there like a little boy frozen by indecision.

Clare came to me, dropped her bag, and embraced me. Neither of us spoke. We just stood in the crowd, holding one another, breathing together. Finally she stepped back, placed her large hands on each of my shoulders, and looked into my eyes…"Lucky, how are you?"

Her eyes were like sunlight. It was hard to look into them.

"I'm ok," I said, "It's really good to see you."

"You too," she said, "We have missed you."

Then something I had never experienced with her before happened, something that is difficult to explain. Her face was the same, but her voice was changed. For just a second, it seemed deeper, as if it were coming from somewhere within her, but beyond her. It was a voice synchronized to the shape of her, and I knew it was the first time I had ever heard Clarence speak.

"We have both missed you," and once again she hugged me.

One of the things that is the hardest for a person who grew up like me is knowing what to do with a hug. It is a non sequitur of physical contact. In church, when we do the "passing of the peace" and people lightly embrace one another in a ritual of caring, I always feel robotic. My shoulders tense. My back stiffens. Like a mechanical man I extend my arms and try to mimic the movements that seem so natural to others. It is not a rejection of human contact, but an unfamiliarity with it. Or perhaps, an over familiarity. I don't know. I have heard psychologists say that those who have been abused in childhood find this closing of the gap of personal space more of a violation than a validation. Maybe. All I know is that it has always made me uncomfortable. Always, until that moment when Clarence hugged me.

It was not the bear hug of the overly zealous male or the bosomy squeeze of the enthusiastic female or the pat-pat of either gender trying to feign closeness. It was an enfolding. It was as if Clare had wings, great golden wings, that encircled me for a moment with warmth, sheltering me from the sounds of the world around me. My own arms reached out to receive this embrace, but I do not remember the sensation of them touching anything but more warmth. I closed my eyes. I drifted in time without space. Then it was over.

"Shall we go?" she asked. It was Clare again.

I shook my head to bring her face back to focus.

"Sure," I stammered, "This way. I have an ATV outside."

On the way into the city, as we glided down Nevsky Propseckt, I pointed out the same sights Digby had shown me when I first arrived. We looked out at the roof top gardens, the windmills, the refineries, the oxy-maker plant. I was glad that the sand storms had decided to take a break so she could see the city clearly. We passed Saint Michael and All Angels.

"Bigger than I thought," was all she said.

I showed her where I lived near the park with its sun shade. We drove on to the best hotel in Burroughs Base, the Princess Anastasia. It was on the far side of Burroughs Base, away from the older parts of the town, with a nice view of the Pathfinder Valley, named after the landing site of one of the earliest Mars probes centuries before.

The Princess Anastasia is a Russian architectural confection, a miniature Winter Palace, with powder blue façade and great arched windows trimmed in white. An imported chandelier hangs like a great jewel in the lobby sparkling in diamond light. The floors are imported mahogany. Golden cherubs seem to hold up the ceiling as they float on curled columns of faux marble. The Princess Anastasia is an echo of elegance from the Empire, brought to Mars like a memory of snow in the desert.

We said good-bye in the lobby. Clare went to her room to rest. I told her I would return that evening for dinner so we could talk before the trial began the next day. She gave me a serious look and took my hand.

"I am so glad I am here, Lucky" she said, "I will be with you…we will be with you…no matter what."

I felt tears push against the dam of my eyes. I tried hard to hold them back. There was so much I wanted to say. So deep a need to apologize. To admit failure. To just break down and ask her to forgive me. But I had lost my voice. All the words had hidden inside me. All I could do was look back at her and understand what she was offering me. She was my friend.

When I got home I was startled as Ima Theresa opened the door. My hang up about hugging took another jolt as she wrapped her arms around me and squeezed. Over her shoulder I saw Beth and Alima standing next to Dr. Wu.

"When did you get back?" I asked, looking past her to see Alima.

"Just about an hour ago," she said. She released me from her arms and I greeted Beth with a polite hug. This was starting to become a pattern.

When I stood before Alima I felt unsure of what to do. My hugging complex was reaching critical overload. Should I embrace her? Would that embarrass her in front of the others?

"A' Salaam Aleykum," she said extending her hand.

"Wa Alekyum a'Salaam" I said and held her hand, "I am so glad to see you again."

"You, as well," she said politely, "Please, meet my brothers."

I turned to see two large men step out of my kitchen. They were both dressed in Martian homespun jackets and trousers. They each wore a kufi, the woven cap of Islam. Even beneath their neatly trimmed black beards I could see they had the same fine features and deep almond eyes of their sister.

"This is Omar and Hassan," she said.

"A' Salaam Aleykum," they both said. I returned their greeting.

"Please, everyone sit down," said Dr. Wu, "Ima Maria, Kalisha and Abba Isidore will soon be back with food, but I know the bishop will want to hear the news."

"Yes," I said, "I do want to hear. Were you able to return uncle Kamil's body to New Medina?"

I sat on the old sofa next to Theresa. Dr. Wu, Billy, Alima and her two brothers took chairs and pulled them around in a rough circle.

"We were able to give my uncle a proper burial," she said, "That was a great relief to the family."

"I'm sure it was," I said, "I will always remember him with great respect."

"Thank you," said Alima quietly.

"As for the MACs," said Ima Theresa, "they did a good job. They recovered several pieces of the two drones and documented the areas where the attack happened. They even holopixed the remains of the camel."

"But did they make any connections to The Vegas?" I asked.

"Not yet," said Ima Theresa, "It seems that the drones were stolen."

"From the Mars Mining Consortium," said Dr. Wu. Ima Theresa nodded.

"But who else could be behind that except The Vegas?" I asked.

"Good question," said Theresa, "and the answer seems obvious. But proving that The Vegas was responsible for the theft will be hard to do. They cover their tracks. Somehow, they learned that you were in the desert. Somehow they stole the drills. Somehow they tracked you. But that's how it always is with The Vegas…a somehow."

We all sat in silence for a moment.

"Could the mining company be involved?" I asked, looking at Dr. Wu. He shrugged.

"Again, it would be hard to prove. They reported the theft some time ago," he said, "I doubt that they are directly involved, but someone could have been paid to leave a door open or look the other way."

"Are the MACs to be trusted?" I asked the questions because in my experience on Earth the cops were only the visible arm of The Vegas.

"I believe so," said Alima, "They are under Imperial authority. Their officer, the one you met at New Medina, seemed very serious about what she was doing."

"I agree," said Ima Theresa, "The Empires don't mind if The Vegas keeps crime organized for them. In fact, they count on it. But if The Vegas did anything that would upset the strict rule of law and order on their own turf, they would come down hard."

I looked at Alima.

"So there is nothing more we can do but wait to see if they can find anything that implicates The Vegas."

"I am afraid so," she said.

I was about to say that I would probably have five years to wait for the outcome, but Ima Maria walked in with Isidore and Kalisha, carrying Chinese takeout. The circle broke up as the food was laid out on the desk. In the confusion I had a moment to speak to Alima alone.

"You didn't have to come," I said, "Ima Theresa could have delivered the news."

"How could I not come when you are about to stand trial for your life?" she said.

"It's only a five year sentence," I corrected her.

Alima looked at me without speaking. She didn't have to say anything. We both knew she was right.

"Did you ever see this?"

Clare handed me a holopix. We were sitting in a quiet corner booth of the restaurant at the Princess Anastasia. I had told her everything that had happened to me since I became the Bishop of Mars. She had told me how it had sent a shock wave back to Earth, shaking the foundations of the church. We both understood that the outcome of the trial would either vindicate us both or sink us. It was that simple.

I looked at the image wavering in the holopix.

"Is this you?"

Clare nodded.

"You were a handsome kid."

The twenty year old boy in the holopix was standing next to a tree, dressed in a tee-shirt and rolled up jeans. He was the kind of kid who could have been groomed by The Vegas to become a heavy-weight boxer, but he had a shy smile.

"He's me," she said, "In more ways than one. I was a shy little girl."

"You two have been together a long time."

Clare switched off the holopix. She took a sip of water.

"We will always be together," she said, "but now, thanks to Clarence, it will be different."

I gave her a quizzical look, "How so?"

"He has decided that it is my turn," said Clare quietly.

As usual, I was at a loss for the right words.

"You will get the change?"

Clare nodded. And then she smiled. And the smile lit up her sunflower eyes into candlelight. I reached over the table to take her hand.

"I am so happy for you," I said, "so happy."

"Me too," she smiled.

"To Clarence," I said spontaneously, raising my water glass, "Thank you, dear Clarence."

"You are welcome," said Clare, or at least, it came from Clare, and those words settled like a benediction around us, enfolding us…all three of us…into a silence of smiles, a moment when words are not needed, when silence alone can express what the heart seeks to say.

The waiter drifted by to see if we wanted more coffee. When he left Clare leaned forward and clasped her large hands on the table.

"Now what are we going to do to win this fight?" she asked, "I have got to find a way to get you out of this mess, but I just don't know how."

"I am afraid there isn't much anyone is going to be able to do. The facts are all against us. The prosecution has an almost airtight case. Dr. Wu has faith that Digby will make a miracle happen. That's about our only hope."

"Well, we believe in miracles."

"You mean, you and Dr. Wu?

"No, I mean me and me." Clare leaned back in the booth. "Listen, Lucky, I am one stubborn nun and one kick-ass older man. I will not give up hope and I will believe God will show us a way."

I smiled, "You know, that's the attitude that saved my life once before when you stayed with me in the hospital"

"And it will again."

Clare's faith seemed to flow into me like fresh air.

"You didn't make this trouble," she said, "You just found it here waiting for you. Either we face it or we look the other way. I think we need to face it."

"No matter what it costs?" I ask.

Clare opened her hands as though she were standing at an altar.

"What good is faith if you don't use it, Lucky?"

And I knew she was right.

Chapter Thirteen

The burning bush had gone out. It was still smoking, but the branches were black fingers of wood. I was standing before it on the orange sand of Mars. I had my shoes off.

"So what do I do now?" I asked.

"You go to court and see what happens," the Bush said.

I wiggled my toes in the sand.

"I don't know," I said, "I'm not so sure that's a good idea."

"What's the matter?" said the Bush, "Don't you trust me?"

"Of course I trust you," I said quickly, "but I could use a little help here."

"You still think you need a miracle?"

"That would be nice," I said.

"I'm all out of plagues," said the Bush.

"Then how about sending someone with me?" I said.

"I sent you Ima Maria," said the Bush.

"I was thinking more of a lawyer."

"I will send you something even better."

"Like what?"

"Like something that no one has ever seen before."

The court room was a large room, with a high vaulted ceiling and a clerestory of primoglass windows that let in a bright light. Rows of benches that reminded me of church pews were separated from the main floor by a low metal railing. These benches were filled with onlookers. Ima Theresa and Beth Ionescu, Dr. Wu, Abba Isidore and Kalisha, Billy, Alima and her brothers, Abba Ambrose, even the black robed Russian priest who had driven me out to the hermitage on my flight to New Medina. I recognized several faces from the diocese. The Saint Vlad steelworkers were there. Some of the artists from Quilong. A few faces from New Shanghai. Only Digby was absent, but Dr. Wu had told me that he had gotten a call and Digby was on his way.

Archbishop Clare sat next to Abba Ambrose. I had seen them talking in the hallway as I came into court with Maria. They seemed so intent on their conversation that I didn't try to speak to Clare. I went in and took my place in the defendant's box.

Across from us, seated in the prosecutor's box, flanked by the two super model lawyers I had seen on the ComCom, was the man with the platinum ring. I suddenly realized that he was the lawyer representing the Mars Central Authority. I looked over at a special area reserved for the Co-Governor's. Both were sitting with placid expressions, one Chinese, one Russian, dressed in the formal black suits of their office. Neither of them looked at me or at the lawyer. Did they know that he worked for The Vegas? Were they in on this deal with him? I rubbed my eyes. I hadn't slept very well the night before and I didn't want to start getting rattled even before the trial began.

"What's wrong?" whispered Ima Maria from her seat next to me.

"Nothing," I whispered back. I could have told her I recognized the lawyer but decided she had enough to worry about. Besides, I wanted her to remain as calm as possible under the circumstances.

And circumstances were bad enough. A MAC bailiff announced "all rise" and the three judges of the Imperial Tribunal entered the courtroom from a side door. We all stood. They mounted some small steps to sit on a raised platform looking down on us. Behind them, crossed on the wall, were the two flags of the Twin Empires. One judge represented the Chinese Empire, the other, the Russian Empire. Seated in the center was a third judge chosen at random, in this case an older Chinese woman with silver hair and a dour expression.

She gaveled the room to silence. We all sat back down and she called for the Prosecutor to make his opening statement.

The case against us was fairly straight forward. The Prosecutor said that it was an open and shut case of disturbing the social order by inciting a riot, causing significant property damage, assaulting officers of the Mars Central Authority and resisting arrest. Ima Maria was named as the instigator. I was named as the one responsible for her actions.

The lawyer then called several witnesses. One by one they filed in to stand before the judges in the witness stand. They were MAC officers. They all told the same story. Ima Maria had led a rabble to the Saint Vladimir City Hall. They had created a disturbance. They had been ordered to disperse. Instead of behaving like law abiding subjects of the Empires they had started a shoving match, trying to gain access to the building. Once inside, things got worse. Chairs were thrown along with punches. A window was smashed. Back up was called. The fight spilled out into the street. Ima Maria had jumped onto the back of a MAC sergeant and had to be pulled off and handcuffed.

I looked over at Maria during this part of the testimony. She was staring down at her lap. I assumed there was no need for me to raise any objections.

After the testimony of the MAC officers, the Prosecutor submitted several holodiscs detailing the property damage, the bruises and cuts suffered by the MACs, and the mug shots of the perpetrators. He offered his summation of the case with a subtle twist to the story.

"Your Honors," he said, "the real crime here was not just the flagrant violation of the law. It was not the disrespect for authority. It was not even the effort to disrupt the social order and peace of Mars by inciting a riot in the streets of one of our major cities. It was also the obvious attempt to intimidate our government from pursuing a course of action whose only intention is to bring prosperity to the Martian community."

He looked meaningfully at the two Co-Governors. They both sat looking back at him with unchanged expressions of deep civic duty.

"Fortunately," he went on, "our officials are above such obvious efforts to extort their leadership. This riot was designed to do what its scurrilous petition had failed to do, force the Mars Central Authority to abandon one of the most important economic investments in the future of Mars ever conceived. Thousands of potential jobs would have been lost. Billions in Imperial currency would have been lost. A vast opportunity for the development of Mars would have been lost. Failing to incite this loss through political pressure, the perpetrators turned to violence. Only through the brave efforts of our Constabulary, who risked their lives to safeguard our rights under the law, these revolutionaries would have continued their plans for social upheaval across the face of Mars."

He looked at Ima Maria and me.

"I shudder to think of the consequences. Hiding beneath the veneer of religion, which in itself should be a crime, these two malcontents plotted an attack on the very foundation of our civilization. It is our duty to send a clear message to all who oppose the peaceful development of our planet that this will not be tolerated. It is our duty to convict them of their crimes to the fullest extent of the law. Unless they are contrite…"

He glanced at me.

"…and prepared to recant their slurs against the government, they must be found guilty and punished with the greatest severity. Only then can loyal subjects of the Empires rest easy in their beds, knowing that progress will not be thwarted by revolutionaries who pose as spiritual guides."

With a dramatic pause, he ended his oration and slowly resumed his seat. I saw the three judges look at one another. Whoever the prosecutor was working for, he had just earned his money. He had succeeded in tying the Mega Mars Project to the case against us with a ribbon of patriotism and a fear of social revolution. He had branded Maria and me as poseurs, faux clergy, who had a secret plan to destroy the future of the planet. The judges were impressed. The Co-Governors were impressed. Most of all, from the smug expression on his face, the lawyer had impressed himself.

Now it was my turn. Almost. First...we heard from my co-defendant.

"Bullshit," she cried, "That's nothing but bullshit."

The Chief Judge banged the gavel.

"You are out of order," said the judge in a loud voice.

"No, he is out of order," cried Ima Maria rising to her feet, "what he just said is a lot of bullshit."

The Judge kept hammering her gavel. One of the bailiffs started walking toward us. The crowd broke out into an excited babble. I grabbed Maria and tried to get her to sit down. She pushed my hands away.

"We aren't revolutionaries," she said waving her arms, "We are priests. We're trying to get justice. We want the Mega Mars Project stopped before it turns Mars into another West Hem."

The bailiff grabbed Ima Maria around her waist. She started swinging her arms at him. Some of the steelworkers were starting to shout.

"Order! Order!" cried the Chief Judge.

More bailiffs entered the room. Some of them tried to calm the crowd. Two more ran over to drag Ima Maria away.

"Justice," she yelled, "Justice! Stop Mega Mars!"

"Take that woman from this court," shouted the Judge.

The bailiffs manhandled Maria out of the room through a side door.

"Stop Mega Mars," were the last words we heard as the door closed behind her.

The Chief Judge banged her gavel three more times.

"I will have order in this court," she said in a loud voice, "I will hold anyone else who speaks in contempt. Am I clear?!"

The room quieted down. The steelworkers awkwardly resumed their seats. I could see Alima looking at me. A bailiff stood next to me in the event that I wanted to join Ima Maria. The Prosecutor just sat in his chair watching me, a small smile tugging at the corners of his mouth.

"This court will stand in recess for thirty minutes," said the Judge, then looking at me, "At that time the defendant will present his case. And there had better be no further outbursts. Am I understood?"

"Yes, Your Honor," I said but my voice was lost in the commotion as the three judges left the chamber and the crowd broke up into a frenzy of conversation.

During the break I walked over to the metal railing to stand in a huddle with my friends. The crowd had shuffled out along with the two Co-Governors and the prosecutor. Except for a bailiff sitting on the far side of the room we were alone. Still, we spoke softly.

"You're screwed," said Ima Theresa, "After that little wild-child performance by Maria, if you don't beg for mercy they are going to throw the book at you. Sorry for being so blunt, but you don't have much time."

No one spoke up to contradict Theresa's graphic summary of my situation.

"I know," I said, "We didn't have much of a defense anyway, but I just cannot say publicly that I am sorry for opposing the Mega Mars Project. That would be wrong."

"Your honor or your freedom," said Dr. Wu, "It is a difficult choice."

"If you are convicted," said Alima, "we can continue the protests. They cannot keep arresting all of us. They will let you go."

"Don't be so sure of that."

It was Clare. The others turned to look at her.

"The stakes are high on both sides," she said, "The Vegas is concerned about losing billions in Imperial currency. They won't stop. The Empires are worried about social order. They won't stop either. If you continue the protests you will only confirm the Prosecutor's argument. You will be seen as revolutionaries and the Mars Central Authority will have to crack down, no matter how many people they need to jail."

"They could declare martial law," said Kalisha.

We all let Kalisha's words hang in the air for a moment. The idea that my decision could not only bring down the church but create chaos on a whole planet covered us with the weight of a reality we could not ignore.

"Listen," I said, "I know what I have to do. There is just no other way out. I can't let you all go down with me so I am going to…"

"Sorry I'm late," said a voice from the back of the huddle, "Did I miss anything?"

It was Digby.

The group parted and he squeezed his way to stand next to the railing. His old overalls were covered in dirt. His goggles sat on top of his head. His face was powdered with a fine dust. It made his eyes look twice as large where the goggles had created circles around them. He rubbed his crew cut hair vigorously and smiled up at me.

"So what has been going on?" he asked again.

We all took turns filling in the story as Digby looked from one person to the next until he had the complete picture.

"So I have made my decision," I said, "I am going to take the fall for this one."

Alima started to speak, but I cut her off.

"There is no other way. I am going to give my speech telling the truth about how rotten this whole deal is and let them put me away. At least I will have done the right thing."

"Not so fast," Digby said, "What you need is a good lawyer."

"We tried to find one," said Abba Isidore, "but it's too late now."

"No it's not," said Digby, "I will take the case."

We all stood frozen for a moment. The doors opened and the crowd began to file back in. Court was about to resume.

"You?" I said quickly, "Digby, are you a lawyer?"

"Not exactly," he said, "I'm Jewish. It's the next best thing. We have been arguing with God for centuries. Trust me."

"Oh brother," said Ima Theresa.

"Excellent idea," laughed Dr. Wu.

Alima took Digby's hand, "Are you sure you know what you are doing?" she asked.

Digby looked at her and spoke with a quiet confidence.

"Yes," he said, "I do. I have spent my entire life looking for something precious. Now, I have found it. It's right here. With all of you. With all of us. This is what I have been looking for. Trust me on this one."

Alima looked toward me. The bailiff was calling for order.

"Let him do it," she said to me.

Clare placed her hand on Digby's shoulder, "We agree," she said, "Let him try."

I quickly surveyed their faces. I nodded and walked back to the defendant's box. Only when the Judges began to file in did it strike me that Digby had never told me he was Jewish.

There were three immediate reactions in the court when I said that Digby would present the case for the defense as my lawyer. The Judges looked down at his dusty overalls with a frown. The Prosecutor looked at him with confusion. The two Co-Governors looked like they had just woken up and were late for work.

The courtroom was silent.

"You may proceed," said the Chief Judge.

Digby stood before the bench and addressed the court.

"Your Honors," he said in a clear voice, "I apologize for my absence from this court during the time that the Prosecutor presented his case. However, I did not need to be present to imagine his argument. I am sure that he told you that my clients created a disturbance that resulted in an unfortunate altercation with MAC officers at the Saint Vladimir City Hall. To this charge, we plead no contest."

There was a murmur of voices through the room. The Prosecutor looked away from Digby and then at me. He was turning his pinky ring like a dial, trying to tune in to where this argument was going.

The Judge tapped her gavel lightly to hush the crowd.

"Are you entering a guilty plea?" she asked.

I saw the two Co-Governors lean forward in their chairs. Digby held up one small, dusty hand.

"No," he said, "We are not. We are not contesting the events that transpired at Saint Vladimir, but we are contesting the circumstances that led up to those events. We are prepared to prove that the motivations behind them were in the best interest of Mars and of enormous value to the government."

Another wave of voices rippled around the room. The Judge tapped her gavel. I had no idea what Digby was saying, but like everyone else in the room I couldn't take my eyes from him.

"Please explain," said the Judge.

Digby extended one hand toward the Prosecutor who was now a study in indecision.

"The Prosecutor has undoubtedly ascribed only the most venal motives to the actions of my clients," he said, "I am sure that he has done his best to frighten this court into believing that they were intentionally fomenting social disorder in order to halt the proposed development of property outside the city limits of Burroughs Base."

Digby paused. The Judges peered down at him from their bench. He had reminded them exactly of what the Prosecutor had claimed. Slowly he reached into a large pocket on his overalls. He pulled out a small canvas bag. He held it up. It seemed to contain something solid.

"I hold in my hand proof that my clients are neither revolutionaries nor obstructionists, Your Honors, but true patriots whose only motivation was the protection of the greatest asset Mars has to offer to the Empires. An asset far more valuable than any casino could ever be."

The crowd came alive again. The Prosecutor jumped to his feet.

"Your Honor!" he shouted, "I object. If there are valuable minerals on the property in question they are included in the contract already established between the purchaser and the government. They cannot justify the actions of the defendants, unless the goal of the defense is to lay claim to them. That would only compound the base motives of Bishop Anthony and his accomplice."

The Judge turned her eye toward Digby.

"Is this your claim?" she asked, "Are you saying that your clients knew of mineral deposits on the land in question?"

Once again Digby paused. Still holding the bag before him he stepped toward the bench.

"No, Your Honor," he said in a hushed voice, but the room was so still it carried clearly for all to hear, "My clients were not concerned to achieve wealth through the discovery of precious minerals on the public lands under question. They were concerned with protecting something far more valuable than gold. They sought to protect the very heritage of Mars itself and its future as well. They sought to protect what I hold in my hand."

If a particle of Martian dust had drifted to the floor in the courtroom that day you could have heard it as the Judge leaned forward to ask Digby, "And what do you hold in your hand?"

Digby removed a brick from the bag and laid it on the judge's bench.

The Chief Judge lifted the brick and examined it.

"It's a brick," she said, "a common Martian brick."

"That is correct, your Honor, a common Martian brick. I found it under the sign that announces the coming of the Mega Mars project."

"I don't understand," said the Judge, "we have made millions of bricks on Mars. What is so special about this one?"

"Just that," said Digby, "*We* didn't make this brick. Not this one and not the thousands more like it under the sands where The Vegas wants to build their casino…the thousands of bricks that constitute an ancient building site. An *alien* building site. *We* didn't make any of them. Someone…or something…else did. They are proof that *we* are not the first Martians."

"I still don't get it," said Ima Theresa, "How could we take credit for discovering aliens on Mars?"

Digby laughed as Billy poured him some more champagne. We were all crowded into my living room, sitting or standing under the watchful eye of Rasputin.

"Because, technically, you did discover it," said Digby, "I would never have gone back to wander around on the Mega Mars site if the bishop had not told me to. I just let the judges think that he had done this on purpose, because you all suspected it was the perfect location to discover proof of an ancient Martian civilization."

"Go back to the beginning," said Dr. Wu.

"That's right," said Digby, I went back to the place where this story began, back to the Mega Mars site where the bishop first had his accident…"

"And first met Alima," I said.

"Exactly," said Digby, "and without realizing it, first stumbled on to where civilization on Mars first began."

"So, there are more bricks under the ground there?" asked Billy.

"Many more," said Digby, "an ancient ruin created long before we ever came to Mars, but built with very much the same basic resources, simple Martian brick."

"By ancient Martians?" Alima asked.

"Perhaps," said Dr. Wu, "but more likely by alien visitors come to Mars long ago, just like human beings. Only time and archeology will tell us the truth."

"Unbelievable," said Ima Maria, "but how did you know to look there?"

"I didn't," admitted Digby, "I didn't look at all. I went out there, closed my eyes, and listened. Just as Dr. Wu advised. I closed my mind to perception and opened it to intuition. And then, I began to hear strange voices in the wind. I followed those sounds and not far from the Mega Mars sign I dug up my first brick."

"It was God's will," said Alima.

"It was a miracle," said Beth.

"It was both," said Clare.

"I agree," said Abba Isidore, "but won't The Vegas still be able to make their deal with the government? Won't they just plow it all up and build their casino anyway?"

"They can't," said Digby, "That land is outside the city limits. It is on Imperial lands. Now it can't be sold because the law forbids them to."

"The Alien Artifact Law," said Clare. Digby nodded.

"The first law on the books when the Mars colony was established," he said, "Any site on Mars that can be proven to show signs of original life automatically becomes an Imperial land reserve, permanently set aside for scientific research. It can't be bought or sold."

"Or developed," I said.

"Exactly," said Digby.

"But what about other property outside the city?" asked Isidore, "What is to prevent The Vegas from buying up any other available space and building their casino?"

"I am afraid there is no more available land near Burroughs Base," said Dr. Wu, "It seems that some wealthy Hungarian has taken possession of it."

"Wow," said Billy, "another miracle."

"Looks like we're up to our ass in miracles around here," said Ima Theresa, holding her glass out for another round, "And God bless the Russians for providing the champagne."

Kalisha began to fill more glasses for the champagne drinkers. Alima went into the kitchen to get sparkling water for her brothers. I followed her so we could have a moment to talk.

"It really does seem like a miracle, doesn't it?" I said, "The Vegas has packed up and gone home. Ima Maria and I have gone from criminals to patriots, thanks to Digby's spin on the story. The Co-Governors are basking in the expectation of a major government research project."

"And you are the Bishop of Mars once again," she smiled.

"Now that's a miracle," I said.

Alima poured water into the glasses. We could hear laughter in the other room. I looked at her.

"Will you go back to New Medina soon?" I asked.

"Yes," she said, "We will leave tomorrow with Beth and Theresa."

"You two have become good friends."

Alima smiled, "I like her," she said, "She is a very honest person."

"I'll miss you," I said quietly.

Alima stopped pouring the drinks and looked at me.

"God brought us together for a purpose," she said softly, "We are only part of that plan."

"To stop the Mega Mars Project?" I asked.

Alima looked away for a moment. The afternoon sun streaming through the kitchen window held her face in hands of light. She looked back at me.

"Yes," she said, "I think that was the role we played. You. Me. Uncle Kamil. All of us. But who knows what other plans God may have for us."

There were several things that I thought of saying, but I decided to just ask, "So we may see one another again?"

Alima gave me a Mona Lisa smile.

"Insha'Allah," said Alima, "Insha'Allah."

Digby was having his holopix made with Alima's brothers when I came back into the living room. Theresa was taking the picture.

"I have a standing invitation to come to New Medina," said Digby.

"Maybe I can come with you," I said.

"You will always be welcomed," said Hassan.

"But not any time too soon," I heard Clare say. I turned to see her standing beside me.

"You have work to do," she said smiling, "You have a diocese to take care of and there's someone here who wants to help."

I looked past her shoulder to see Abba Ambrose standing like a black flag in the center of the room. He was holding something under his arm, but he extended his other hand.

"I have come to congratulate you," he said. The room had gone quiet as the others watched to see what my reaction would be.

I stepped forward and clasp his hand warmly in mine.

"Thank you, Abba," I said, "I appreciate that very much. It will be good to work with you again."

Abba Ambrose nodded and then held up the gift he had been holding by his side.

"This is for you," he said, "a gift from Saint Michael and All Angels. A token of our support to you as our bishop."

I held up the painting. It looked vaguely like a work I had seen before in The Vegas museum in Pilgrim's Palace, the only piece of fine art in the whole exhibit. It was called *The Scream* by Edvard Munch. The Vegas must have liked the painting because it showed a man with a distorted head screaming on a bridge. This new painting from Mrs. Quigly looked a lot like it, only in this version the screamer was wearing a blue veil.

"The Blessed Virgin Mary," said Abba Ambrose, "to go with your portrait of Jesus."

"What can I say?" I stammered, "Words escape me."

That night I drove Clare back to the Princess Anastasia. It was cold and we were bundled up in Digby's beat up old ATV as we bounced along the road to the hotel. The party had broken up and all the guests had gone their separate ways. Theresa, Beth and Billy were returning to Quilong. Alima and her brothers would go with them and then travel on to New Medina. Dr. Wu was back in his garden, listening to his plants. Isidore and Kalisha were driving home to New Shanghai, holding hands in the happy knowledge that all had turned out well. Abba Ambrose was carrying my deep thanks to Mrs. Quigly for her gift that now hung on my wall next to Rasputin. Digby had gone… well…Digby had just gone to wherever Digby goes.

Clare and I drove in silence until we came to the hotel. She asked me to park and walk out onto the veranda to take one more look at the night sky before she turned in to get some sleep for her early morning flight to Home World.

We stood looking out at the Martian desert, bathed under the pale light of the twin moons that raced across a field of stars. Our breath made little clouds in the chill evening air.

"It truly is beautiful," said Clare, "I envy you the chance to make this your home."

"I'm grateful to you for giving me that chance," I said, "I think I will find what I have been looking for here."

Clare turned to look at me. Her eyes were faded to a soft yellow in the moonlight.

"You've found some very good friends here, Lucky."

"More than friends," I said, "They feel like family."

She nodded.

"Like I found with my Sisters."

She reached in her shoulder bag.

"Before I go, I have two gifts for you." She pulled a long woolen scarf from the bag and draped it around my neck. "First, the scarf from Sister Margaret. The Sisters are worried that you will catch cold on Mars."

I lifted up the ends of the dark blue scarf, admiring it.

"Thank you," I said, "And thank Sister Margaret and all the Sisters."

Next she took out the holopix she had shown me at dinner. It was the picture of Clarence.

"Just something to remember me by," she said, "When you see me next, I will be Clare."

I looked at the shy boy in the white tee-shirt.

"Thank you so much, Clarence, this means a great deal to me," I looked at her, "And you mean a great deal to me, Clare. I will always love you both."

Without another word she leaned over and kissed me on the cheek.

She said goodnight and walked inside. I watched her disappear into the gilt and gold of the Princess Anastasia.

It was getting cold, but I stayed on the veranda for a while longer, watching Mars sleep. I pulled my new scarf snug against my neck. I held Clare's picture in my hand. I looked into the night sky. Between